# The Mystical Milestone

*A novel dedicated to my father Will and my mother Katie. They were proud people, in the good sense of the word, and sacrificed much for me.*

First impression: 2014

© Peter Griffiths & Y Lolfa Cyf., 2014

ISBN: 978 1 84771 827 3

Published and printed in Wales
on paper from well-maintained forests by
Y Lolfa Cyf., Talybont, Ceredigion SY24 5HE
*e-mail* ylolfa@ylolfa.com
*website* www.ylolfa.com
*tel* 01970 832 304
*fax* 832 782

# The Mystical Milestone

## Peter Griffiths

y Lolfa

# THANKS TO:

Ardy Cardwell who enthused at a crucial time.

Janet Watkins Masoner (Sianed) who encouraged and advised.

Elin Lewis who edited with a combination of rigour and flexibility.

Leighton Phillips who, through his company Graphicwave, designed my website – www.themysticalmilestone.com – with imagination, patience, and promptness.

Ac yn olaf i Lefi o'r Lolfa.

# Author's Notes

This novel serves to highlight the Gower Peninsula which, in 1956, became the first area in the United Kingdom to be designated an Area of Outstanding Natural Beauty.

The picture on the front cover is the lych-gate of Llangennydd church. The church, which is in the background, is the largest in Gower and the only one with a lych-gate. Quoting *Chambers Dictionary*, "lych" is a body, living or dead, and "lych-gate" is a roofed churchyard gate to rest the bier under.

The picture on the back cover is of Worm's Head, Rhossili Bay, Gower.

On the next page there are two maps. The upper one puts the Gower Peninsula in perspective, and the other is a close-up of it.

All characters in the novel are fictional.

Rhossili is pronounced "Ross … illy (as in hilly)".

As for Llangennydd, "Ll" is impossible to describe, the "g" is hard, the "y" is pronounced as a short "i" and the "dd" as a soft "th".

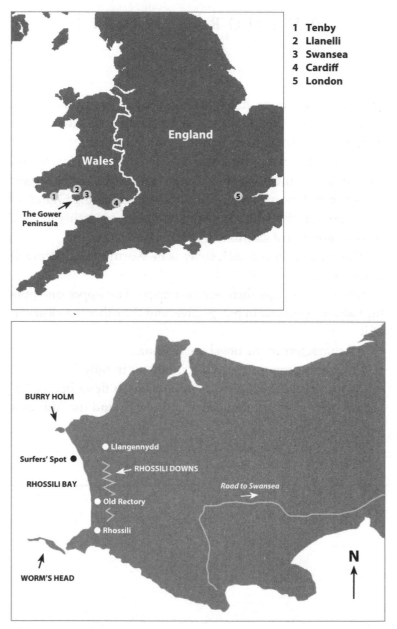

1 Tenby
2 Llanelli
3 Swansea
4 Cardiff
5 London

England

Wales

The Gower Peninsula

BURRY HOLM

Surfers' Spot ●

RHOSSILI BAY

● Llangennydd

← RHOSSILI DOWNS

*Road to Swansea* →

● Old Rectory

● Rhossili

WORM'S HEAD

N

**Western end of Gower**

# ONE

DURING THE SUMMER, Rhossili, a village on the south-west corner of Gower, is a tourist trap. Its appeal rests on startling views – weather permitting, a breathtaking beach, iconic Worm's Head – a distinctive promontory, and a world's end feeling that is synonymous with sheer cliffs at the tips of peninsulas.

Arthur and Peggy Harris lived in the upper part of the village from where they enjoyed a panorama of the Bristol Channel and its jewel Lundy Island. Arthur had an older sister Mrs Maggie Williams who lived just two doors away with her husband Trevor. A recently retired and experienced gynaecological nurse, Mrs Williams was highly respected by Peggy's GP and pivotal to his decision to allow Peggy, at forty years of age, to have her firstborn at home. As it happened the birth was straightforward, and the baby named Annie; the year was 1960, the day July 20th.

Mrs Williams was pleasingly stocky. She nursed the newborn, merely an hour old, and smiled sympathetically at the mother who was half asleep.

"Poor thing! Peggy looks so tired, but she's still pretty," mused Mrs Williams, whose face was pretty too and not dissimilar to her sister-in-law's… just rounder, with a slightly receding brow and topped with grey.

"Peggy's so petite," she continued, "but she's strong as well… and exceptionally nice, which is just as well, living with that touchy brother of mine. I don't know how she puts up with him. Can you imagine? He can never admit that he's wrong, he can never say that he's sorry, and to make matters worse he's so quick to take offence, and few of them are forgotten. He's been that way since I remember. Insecure, I've always thought."

Mrs Williams gazed with admiration at Annie.

"You've got your father's features, darling, and your Auntie Maggie's as well, I suppose," and then, reflectively, "This baby's been a long time coming. Peggy really deserves her, and of course by now they've got money to bring her up… properly. You've got to give Arthur his due. He doesn't make much as a bus driver but sticking with his car repair business has certainly paid off."

She smiled fondly at Peggy and then spoke in a whisper to Annie.

"Because you look like your father, perhaps there's a good chance you'll grow up to be like your mother. Let's hope so anyway… fingers crossed!"

It was obvious to everyone that Annie was a happy little girl, and each time she smiled, a dimple came to life on her left cheek. Annie was pretty too and eye-catching in her pigtails and generally colourful clothes. At school she was regularly praised, and whenever the tranquillity of her world was threatened by an event, a dream or dark thoughts, she confided in her mother who soothed her.

As her self-awareness grew, however, she found herself too ashamed to reveal some concerns. Not even her mother would be told of Annie's envy for another girl who seemed so natural in the company of boys. She bottled this negative emotion and stewed, unable to place her feelings in perspective. Rather than be pleased for a girl who was natural at little else, Annie established her as a threat.

Annie was thirteen before she fully understood that when doubts surfaced, they disturbed her much more than they did other people. When bothered by an issue, she usually found it hard to shake off immediately. She couldn't dismiss it and get on with things as others seemed to be able to do: she obsessed over it, and it weighed on her. For example, when she was fourteen she had a boyfriend... of sorts... who seemed to enjoy complimenting other girls. Annie took this in her stride until one of his comments about another girl did stick in her mind and she began to wonder whether her boyfriend liked her less than he did the other girl. Annie knew this to be improbable, but she couldn't shelve the notion; nor, to make matters worse, could she prevent images of the girl from interrupting unrelated trains of thought. Eventually, something was said or done which enabled Annie to put things in better perspective. She failed, however, to derive encouragement from such resolutions, setting herself up for regular repeats of the process.

At another time, she agreed to play the piano in a school concert. As on similar occasions in the past, she worried unduly that she'd let herself down on stage. She never had and nor did she this time, so what a pity to have expended so much energy in imagining the worst. Annie found it hard not to dwell on doubt, her glass alas half empty. Annie's inability to control her thoughts and her tendency to obsess over the slightest hiccup drained her of self-esteem. During these early teenage years, Annie lived life on the back foot, much of the time either wrestling with an obsession... or dreading the onset of the next one. She knew that when it came she would recognise it immediately, for a wave of tension would wash her stomach... and then settle there. Her daily routine would prove doubly difficult and her sleep would often suffer, but amazingly she always managed to cope: she really did have grit. Eventually logic, probably laced with luck, would put her mind at rest.

The ensuing relief, however, would be tempered by anger at her inability to control her thought processes. Ashamed of her weakness, pride prevented her from sharing her predicament with a friend or her mother. Surely they'd think less of her, which would be hard to take for one who thought little enough of herself already.

Auntie Maggie had been right when she'd surmised that her brother Arthur's touchiness stemmed from insecurity. Unfortunately, it seemed his daughter had inherited that trait, although its manifestation in her differed greatly from that in her father.

Annie often thought with sadness of how carefree she'd been as a little girl; she wondered what had happened between then and now.

"Where have I gone wrong? Perhaps it's not all my fault, though… it could be out of my control."

Now and then Annie walked along the cliffs towards Worm's Head. On one such walk she was struck out of the blue by the notion of the wind as her friend; she imagined herself being embraced by it… and protected. How thrilling it was to feel connected; her spirits soared. She relished this feeling until suddenly something intangible punctured it. Her let down was hard to take: one minute her mind released, the next uneasy again.

"Will that feeling come back?" she wondered.

When two months later it did, the disappointment which ensued was deeper still.

"It's not worth it," she thought, "I hope it doesn't happen again,"… and it didn't.

So Annie's life was fraught with uncertainty. A typical teenager would likely have found her circumstances debilitating, but Annie fought, and though she often cried, she never gave up. Whenever at her lowest, she would grit her teeth and clench her fists; that seemed to help sustain her as did her dogged determination to do well at school. Her success in most endeavours helped buoy her spirits and offset her extreme insecurity. At those times when she felt light-hearted, Annie had the habit of singing as she went about her business, as if to convince herself that she was happy. It certainly convinced others of the same. Then suddenly, an irrational fixation would put her down again.

Despite these daunting challenges, Annie excelled in her O-level exams. She took them just before her sixteenth birthday; her results were the best in her class. Naturally, her parents were proud, but they'd no clue what anguish she'd suffered... and still did. It's sobering how little we know of each other!

Then, to Annie's surprise, things took a turn for the better. The boost to her self-esteem provided by her O-level results seemed to have snapped her out of her cycle of gloom. And yet, she wasn't out of the woods. It's just that now she found that threats to her peace of mind were usually deflected more easily, and even when they consumed her, they were overcome more readily; doubt was no longer the devil it had been.

The nice thing was that Annie felt more normal and thought better of herself. In consequence, it became easier to be generous to others. More often than not as she walked towards Worm's Head, she did so now with a friend; on several occasions even with the girl who once had been a threat for being so natural around boys.

At eighteen years of age, Annie was considered to be striking and a girl who had it all together; she'd managed to keep her deep-seated flaws to herself. Annie sailed into the university at

Swansea; she had wondered whether to study maths but settled instead for science.

Annie first met Dylan O'Kinnon on a wet, windy morning in Swansea, purportedly the wettest city in Britain; if that were so, quipped many who called it home, then Swansea was the driest wettest city in the world. It was early May, and Annie's first summer term at the university. She drove from home daily and that morning she'd parked her Saab at the seafront as usual. Now, she was hurrying to the main university building with Angus. Also from Rhossili and in his third year, he'd hitched a lift with her. To Annie, it seemed Angus knew everybody, but there was one he greeted particularly warmly. Annie was introduced, and the three walked together the rest of the way. Later that afternoon on their way back to the car, the rain still falling but lightly now, Angus asked, "Well, Annie, did you like Dylan?"

"That's a funny question, Angus!"

"No, really! Did you like him?"

"I don't know!" she protested, "He's good looking and personable. So, I suppose, yes; I did like him. Why d'you ask?"

"Because he likes you, that's all."

"Come off it, Angus!" blushing slightly, "How d'you know that, anyway? Did he tell you?"

"No! He didn't have to tell me. I just knew by the way he behaved this morning. I know him well, and he's normally very light and tongue in cheek, but with us this morning, well… he was different. I think you made an impression, Annie."

In the Saab now, all set to get Angus and his backpack to his digs.

"I'd get to know him, Annie, if I were you. He's one of

the leaders of the rugby team, you know, and he's not too bad at cricket either. He'd open all kinds of doors for you, I promise."

"Angus, you're being totally ridiculous," from Annie angrily, "I've spent five minutes with him, for goodness sake," and then more calmly, "anyway, he's too old for me, and I'm not keen on rugby types."

"Oh! He's not like that. He's sociable, of course, but he's not one of the lads... not a rowdie at all. Dylan's a nice chap, Annie; sensitive too... and very loyal."

As she approached a tight roundabout, Annie asked triumphantly, "So, why doesn't he have a girlfriend then if he's so attractive?"

"Well, maybe he does, but he's about to make a change."

"Angus, you're terrible! Let's drop it now, all right? I'm really not interested."

As she left Angus, Annie was pensive, her forehead furrowed.

"Of course I liked him," Annie whispered to herself in the car, and then in her thoughts, "But what's the point? Why would he like me, anyway? And even if he did, I know what would happen then because it's happened a few times before... and why should this be any different?"

Annie had settled into a routine at the university, coping tolerably well with onsets of doubt, bouts of obsession and her innate insecurity. When presented, however, with this unpredictable situation which involved emotions, she regressed, immediately fearing the worst.

"Why am I even thinking about him?"

Annie was at home by now, preparing to study for an hour before supper.

"He's not going to ask me out. At least I won't have to worry about what would happen after that."

But Dylan did ask her out; Angus was the go-between. Annie was over the moon; for the time being her excitement pushed aside her fears.

Annie met Dylan for dinner in Mumbles. She'd told her parents she'd be home later than usual... and gave the reason: her mother was overjoyed, and her father's predictable suspicions allayed on being told of Dylan's sporting credentials. She sat next to Dylan at a table in a corner of the cafe; her eyes were brown, his very blue; her eyebrows delicate, his prominent; her lips well formed, his much thinner; her hair brown, short of shoulder length, shiny, and immaculately parted... his hair brown as well, but already thinning although he was only twenty-two.

To Annie, Dylan was everything that Angus had said he'd be... certainly nice and sensitive. Above all, she found him gentle, belying the build of a rugby player. It was obvious to Annie that he liked her a lot; this made her glow inside. She drove home that night knowing that something special had been sparked, but not for long did she dwell on this thrilling prospect before her fears of the future took hold. She knew what would happen next; events would unfold in the exact same way as they had in an earlier relationship: during the next few weeks, Dylan would say or do something innocent which would plant a seed of doubt in her mind; she would fail to shake it off; it would mushroom irrationally out of control and dominate her thoughts, especially those involving Dylan; in the end it would sour their relationship. It had happened before, it would happen again... but this time it didn't. Unjustifiable doubts did arise as predicted, but failed to gain traction. That Dylan was consistently attentive, affectionate and sensitive had an immediate and profound effect on Annie. She quickly grew to trust him; in the process, her insecurity faded. She became convinced that Dylan would never do anything to hurt her; in the face of certainty, silly doubts were snuffed out. In fact, Dylan's generosity and devotion had the same beneficial effect as her O-level results: the healing process which they'd begun was reinforced by him.

Annie couldn't remember the last time she'd felt truly happy. Now that she did, she couldn't believe it would last, and in fact a shadow soon descended. It seemed to her that their close – and open – relationship demanded that she disclose her history of obsessing; she began to feel a fraud for not doing so.

"But I can't tell him; it's bound to put him off me!"

For once, her temperament did Annie a favour. She knew that not telling would weigh on her, would dog their relationship… and possibly ruin it. In light of this, what did she have to lose by coming clean?

Two weeks to the day of their first rendezvous, and in the same cafe, Annie bared her soul for the first time since childhood. All the while she held Dylan's hands and his gaze. Early on, he interrupted.

"But we all go through bad patches, Annie; it's part of life."

"No, Dylan, it was worse than that. For a few years, fear dominated my life," and she resumed her story. Towards the end she said, "No wonder I felt depressed at times, but I'm much, much better now," and as she smiled, "thanks to you."

Dylan shook his head deliberately. Still holding her hands and oblivious to the other patrons, he knelt by Annie, caught her gaze, and said, "Jesus, Annie, you've got guts! You've no idea how much I admire you for that." As Annie's eyes misted over, she smiled at Dylan for ages… and all he did was smile at her in return.

Eventually, "Let's have another beer."

Annie often wondered how much pain she'd have spared herself had she opened up earlier in her life. The circumstances would have been different, so who knows what would have happened, but it didn't matter anymore, anyway: the important thing now was that she felt as normal as she had when she was a little girl.

A few weeks later, early in June, Dylan mentioned that he was keen to do well in his accountancy finals; he had only three weeks to go.

"It's not in me to wing it, Annie. I have to be well prepared for me to be relaxed taking these exams, so d'you mind if I see less of you?"

"Well, of course I do, Dylan, but you should do what's best for you."

A few days later Annie had something important to say. They were ambling along Swansea's readily accessible and underrated beach which formed a segment of a majestic bay that swept eastward from Mumbles to Porthcawl. This arc was reminiscent of the Bay of Naples, if one could only ignore a prominent industrial belt, the sea's forbidding hue and a climate prone to rain. Of course, on a warm, cloudless summer's night, one could… and did; Swansea became Napoli, and Porthcawl became Capri.

Annie began with, "Dylan, you do know that I love you, don't you?"

"Yes, Annie, I do," in good humour.

"Even though I do love you, I haven't made love to you, have I?" with an emphasis on "made".

"Not that I know of, Annie," obviously trying to make light of the matter.

"Dylan, I hope you understand why such a step isn't as easy for me as for other people. I'm sorry but I'm just not ready yet. I can tell that you are," and here she smiled, "and that makes me sad, but... but will you leave it up to me? Will you let me decide... please?"

He nodded and, laughing, said, "I'm better off concentrating on my exams for the moment, anyway."

A little later, Annie asked, "Why didn't you have a girlfriend that first time I met you?"

"Because I was waiting for you, Annie," he said, and then smiled provocatively.

"You weren't," she scoffed.

"Well, the way I feel now, I know I was."

Annie laughed. They then held hands and resumed their ambling.

His final examinations over, all Dylan and Annie wished for now was time together. Dylan's mother was persuaded to phone Peggy Harris and invite Annie to their home in Tenby for a fortnight. From Rhossili, with the aid of binoculars, Tenby's colourful frontage can be seen beyond Carmarthen Bay, but to Annie's father it was worlds away. His blessing would have been essential to Annie in the past, but this time she'd determined to go regardless. Perhaps sensing a change in the rules of play, Arthur eventually gave way, but not without regularly reminding his wife that any unfortunate consequence would be her responsibility.

Annie loved Tenby; no underrated beaches there. She loved Dylan's parents too; with them, she felt few inhibitions and revelled in their approval of her. Relieved of lectures and university deadlines, Annie was living a fantasy, one in which she knew her relationship with Dylan would soon be made complete. At last she felt ready to make love to him. She was surprised at how relieved she felt; she was excited too and she saw that Dylan could tell. The moment came on a camping trip along the Pembrokeshire coast. Dylan's father had all the gear, and with his help they'd planned an unambitious schedule. Annie was emotional as they set off in brilliant sunshine… four days alone together! In this exalted mood, to her, Dylan seemed gentler and kinder than ever and the coastline unimaginably beautiful. They'd started late and then dawdled, so camp wasn't made till six. Their site faced west and hung above the sea. As the tent was erected they touched and felt and fondled, childishly. Over dinner at a local pub, they pressed close and playfully kissed. On the walk back she hung on his arm, and for the first time on such an occasion Annie felt no guilt. She was as excited for Dylan as she was for herself. Would she be disappointed? She needn't have wondered: pleasure she was bound to gain for all that she gave in the tent. Outside, breakers broke… for hours.

Dylan became articled to the local office of a large accounting firm, and rented a flat in Mumbles. Because he'd ruled out serious rugby he had more time on his hands than before. Annie, however, could not take advantage of it on account of her study load and having to go home each night. She became discontented; after those four blissful days with Dylan in Pembrokeshire, nothing less would do. With discontent came visitations of her former insecurity; none were overwhelming but they were disconcerting all the same. When she mentioned this to Dylan, she experienced immediate relief. This was a stark reminder of his importance to her well-being and confirmation to her that the more he was a part of her life, the more grounded she would be. Her reaction was obvious, if impetuous: she decided that she would move into Dylan's flat in Mumbles. He was agreeable and excited of course, but advised Annie to seek her parents' blessing. She approached them with conviction: her father's reaction was predictably negative.

"Forget it, Annie, and anyway, you haven't known him for long."

"Long enough to know, Daddy, that I don't want to be with anyone else."

"But you won't be able to study with Dylan around all the time, and your future depends on getting a good degree."

"He's got exams to take as well, you know!"

In dismay, Arthur turned to his wife. She held her daughter's hand as she reasoned, "Aren't you still a bit young to be taking this kind of decision? What if it doesn't work out?"

"Then I'll come home again, but it will work, believe you me, Mammy."

At that, Arthur glared at his wife and whined, "That holiday was a huge mistake. I knew it from the start."

Raising her hands in exasperation, Annie left the room. Both parents looked alarmed, but then one deliberated while the other dug in.

"Arthur, to some extent I feel the same as you. I am surprised though: this isn't like her but she's obviously deadly serious. There's conviction in her voice, and if we don't handle this right, I'm afraid that she'll move in with him, anyway."

"If she does, I'll disown her."

"If you do, I'll disown you."

Not often had Peggy bet the bank like this. As on such previous occasions, she was drilled by his piercing brown eyes, left alone without a word and ostracised for days. Peggy begged Annie to keep an open mind and give her time to reason with her husband. Her entreaties paid off, for a few days later at breakfast, to Peggy's amazement, Arthur said casually, "Dylan is a good boy, isn't he?"

Not a moment did she waste.

"He's a lovely boy, Arthur. Annie couldn't do better."

"And, after all, she was open with us. I'm telling you though, if she hadn't been up front I wouldn't budge an inch."

So there it was. Peggy left well alone; she didn't say another word. But why the change in him, she wondered? This time, she must have spoken with more conviction, which allied to Annie's fearless stand had perturbed Arthur. In any case, seemingly from naught a compromise was wrought. Annie agreed to spend only the weekends with Dylan in Mumbles. No one was fazed by Arthur's parting shot.

"I'm not entirely comfortable with this, Annie, you understand."

# Two

D YLAN SAT ERECT on a blanket while his two young children
played on the grass a few yards away. Every now and then
he shook his head slowly as if in disbelief at a recurring thought.
Soon, Annie approached from the village, clearly excited to see
her family. In a few moments, after hugging her children, she,
on her knees with a child in each arm, turned towards Dylan
and smiled broadly; this encouraged the barely detectable
dimple on her left cheek to come to life. Still bubbly, she asked,
"And how are you, Dylan?"

He smiled as he shrugged his shoulders.

"What's the matter?"

"Listen Annie, let's get going on the picnic first. I bet the
children are starving, and I can tell you what happened while
we eat."

"No, no, no! Please tell me now; I'm sure the children are
fine."

He seemed relieved at her insistence.

"It's just that I had another of those," and here he hesitated,
"episodes with your father."

"Oh, dear! What was it this time?"

"Well, remember the joke about Worm's Head? I told it to
your parents this morning. I walked the children round there,
see, just after you left for Swansea. Well, your father didn't
get the joke. I don't know why: he's usually pretty with it. He
couldn't have been concentrating, I suppose. Your mother,
though, was laughing her head off. You can imagine how that

ticked him off, but he didn't show it until I pitched in stupidly with, 'You're a bit obtuse this morning, Arthur.' Then, in a bad temper, he said, 'You couldn't have said the joke properly, that's all.' Now, I'm not an idiot – I know when to stop, so I didn't say anything more. But he wouldn't let it go, would he? He went on and on about how I couldn't have said it right, and given that, how dare I call him obtuse. He went on and on until I agreed with him in the end just to shut him up."

With her lips now tightened and her mood subdued, Annie shook her head in commiseration, and releasing the children, shuffled close to him, straddled his outstretched legs, and sat on his thighs. They hugged each other, and then she rested her head on his shoulder.

"What a shame," she half-whispered, "but you normally come out of these spats with him smelling like a rose. You've got a light touch with people, Dylan, and especially with him. What went wrong?"

"I just think he took me by surprise, because he's been more reasonable recently, hasn't he? So I wasn't on my toes, I suppose. I don't know if I'll ever hear the end of this one, Annie. You should have seen his face."

Annie leant away from him and, fixing on his very blue eyes, asked with a chuckle, "So, apart from that, Dylan, how was your morning?" and then turning her head towards the sea, said, "And what about you, Connie? You look as pretty as a flower, and doing so well looking after Connor."

Connor, two years old, and Connie, almost four, smiled similarly as only brother and sister could; the only difference being that Connie's smile was a little big for her face. Both children were on the chubby side with fine, fair hair. Connor pushed himself to his feet and sought his sister's hand before running to his mother.

"I bought each of you a present in Swansea," said Annie, "but I left them at the house. I almost didn't tell you, but don't you think it's a good thing that you can look forward to getting them?"

The children gazed up at her with expressions which were surprisingly calm, as if they understood and approved of her philosophy. All four seemed at ease with themselves and each other as they unpacked the rucksack which Dylan had brought along with the blanket.

After the picnic, Connor fell asleep and Connie contentedly coloured a page in her scrapbook. It was a Saturday in early June, 1986, and warm for that time of the year. Dylan had set his blanket a safe distance from the cliff edge. To their right, the white-coated cottages and houses of Rhossili were scattered on an upward slope, and to their left, the crest of Worm's Head peeked over the cliff line. Not far behind them lay a wide and often busy path; the view seaward was sensational. Under slow-moving, unthreatening clouds, Dylan and Annie lay on the blanket side by side; their heads rested on the backpack and they held hands.

"Dylan?"

"Yes, darling?"

"I wish you weren't going to Marlborough tomorrow. I know you'll be back on Wednesday, but… but I always miss you when you're away."

Her brow furrowed at the same time as a cloud obscured the sun.

"Oh, come on now, Annie!"

"I can't help it, Dylan."

He stroked her hand repeatedly and stopped only when she responded by squeezing his, as if that was a signal that she'd overcome her disquiet. As they lay in silence, waves broke, gulls remonstrated and hikers murmured on the pathway. In a while, both sat up and smiled at each other warmly and confidently, brown eyes locked on very blue. Soon after, they headed home to a bungalow opposite the church.

# THREE

THE HOT TUB bubbled and babbled and gave pleasure; a perfect end to Dylan's day in Marlborough. Arms outstretched along the rim of the tub, he relaxed, happy at the thought of being with Annie the following evening. It was half past nine. Someone else had just entered the hotel's fitness room and was preparing to exercise. Several yards from the tub, and facing Dylan, a plain but extremely well-proportioned young woman laid a towel on the floor. She then ran through her yoga repertoire in outrageously inappropriate attire, so as she stretched and swivelled, a baggy blouse barely held her breasts, and her shorts, brief and loose, revealed shadows... some dark and others darker still.

"What the hell's going on here?" Dylan thought, laughing to himself, "Is she just a show-off or am I being blatantly seduced? I wish Annie was here to see this."

Intriguingly, the woman remained deadpan and seemingly oblivious to the mayhem her moves may cause. Initially amused, but now excited by this show of shadows and light, Dylan became aroused... and mildly uncomfortable for he wished for no part of this; so while this yogic Yin did arouse, no Yang would she find in him. Then she stopped and relaxed on the floor. Soon, Dylan stepped out of the tub, dabbed himself with a towel, picked up his bag, and left.

The lift was long in coming. Eventually, it chimed. As Dylan stepped inside, he noticed out of the corner of his eye the woman hurrying out of the fitness room. He needn't have waited, but how petty not to. He was rewarded with a thank you, a seductive whiff of perfume and a close-up of her attributes. Dylan pressed a button and turned enquiringly to her.

"I'm on the same floor, thanks."

While he waited for the door to close, it would have been surprising had Dylan not dwelt, even lightly, on the show of shadows and light. He waited and dwelt... till he realised that the door wasn't closing. The button was pressed again and again until suddenly the door slammed shut. The lift rumbled into action, cleared a floor or more, and jerked violently to a halt. Every button that might have helped was pressed, but to no avail. Dylan turned to the woman.

"Don't worry now. There's an emergency phone here."

Although the lift looked old and had sounded even older, he got through to somewhere. The ringing was encouraging... for a while.

Then, out of the blue, "Hello! May I help you?"

Dylan was taken aback.

"Yes... yes! We're stuck in the lift."

It soon became clear that he was through to a central answering service. He gave the name of the hotel and his opinion that the lift was between the first and second floors.

"Is everyone all right?" he was asked.

"Are you all right?" asked Dylan, turning to the woman; she nodded.

"Yes! We're fine."

"Good! Someone will be with you before long."

"Excuse me," blurted Dylan, "What d'you mean by before long?"

"Five or ten minutes it usually takes."

"Thank you."

Dylan turned to the woman again; her face was not so plain when she smiled. That's when the lights went out... with a flash!

The woman squealed. Dylan squared up to a mild anxiety and reassured.

"It'll only be five minutes, don't worry."

"Oh, you are gallant…"

Was she being sarcastic? Alarm bells tinkled in his brain when a siren would have served him better.

"… but I am very frightened. Would you hold me? I know that would make me feel better. D'you mind?"

Of course he minded, but before he could articulate his thoughts she bumped into him; her arms embraced him and squeezed lightly. This was preposterous, but somehow, involuntarily, perfume and the pressure and warmth of her body led again to thoughts of shadows and light, and once more he became aroused.

"Oh, God! This is so embarrassing. She's bound to feel me; what can I do? I can't help it!"

Perhaps not, but she certainly could as her hand moved slowly down his stomach. Looking back, it was obvious that's when he should have stopped her; and of course he would have… if it hadn't been for her warm-up show; if the lights hadn't failed; if she hadn't said she was frightened. If, if, if… and one may add, if it hadn't at that moment felt so good. But, looking back, even he may be forgiven for not owning up to that. In any case, there were too many ifs… Dylan dithered. Her hand had settled, and what was good became better.

Generally, ecstasy, even when unwelcome, clears the mind of competition, but for some reason while riding this wave of mounting pleasure, it occurred to Dylan that he'd arranged for Annie to phone around this time. The thought drained him of eroticism and snapped him to his senses. This woman was out of her mind; such effrontery on her part, but he had acquiesced. He should have stopped her at the start… but hadn't. Why on earth had he not? Regardless, he now grabbed her head firmly, carefully pushed her away, adjusted his trunks, and wrapped his towel around them. Then, he waited... on alert. Eventually, the emergency phone rang, followed immediately by thumping on the door.

"Are you all right in there?"

Dylan was asked to assist in wedging open the door. He wrapped the towel more tightly around his waist.

In the meantime, Annie had phoned and left a message. Dylan sprawled on his bed, wondering what to tell her.

"Just tell her the truth. You always do."

Strange as it may seem for a man of the world, a one-time rugby star and now already a successful accountant, the most precious aspect of Dylan's life was his relationship with Annie; it gave him lightness. Its basis was trust; they told each other everything, although nothing of this nature had arisen before. His closeness to Annie would complicate Dylan's decision. Most in his position would have instinctively settled for, "I don't have anything to worry about; she'll never find out, and what the eye doesn't see, the heart doesn't grieve."

Dylan, however, debated with himself.

"You stopped the woman in the end. Yes, I know, but I should have stopped her much earlier. How do I explain that to Annie?"

He reasoned that there were powerful extenuating circumstances: everything seemed to have ganged up on him and the woman was nuts, and yet the plain fact was that should the same circumstances coalesce again, he would resist from the very start. He couldn't explain why he hadn't this time.

"If I tell Annie, she's certain to think less of me. If I don't,

I'm bound to be uncomfortable when I'm with her... at least for a while."

Dylan became angry with himself.

"How could I have been so stupid? I didn't want to have anything to do with that woman."

It wasn't until he stopped thinking of his own situation and put himself instead in Annie's shoes that he settled for not telling. Why should Annie share in the fallout of his folly? If he told her, not only would he suffer... from her disfavour... but so would she... from knowing that he'd let her down.

His decision made, he phoned.

"Hello, Annie! I'm really sorry I wasn't here when you rang, but I was stuck in a lift... with the lights out."

"You must be joking!"

"No! It's true."

"Was there anybody with you?"

"No... no there wasn't."

Immediately, he regretted the lie: it had been unnecessary. He could have comfortably told her more of the truth.

"Oh! You poor thing! That must have made it so much worse," and eventually, "I can't wait to see you tomorrow, Dylan."

"Same here, Annie."

He hoped it hadn't sounded lame.

He awoke late, too late for breakfast. This was a relief: the last thing he wanted was to see that woman again. The thought of her reminded him of the discomfort he might feel in Annie's presence for a while.

# FOUR

DYLAN'S DRIVE HOME was uneventful. Each time the episode in the lift came to mind he did experience guilt, but not unduly so; after all, he hadn't sought a liaison and he'd stopped the woman in the end. His overriding emotion was anger, directed at himself.

"How could I have been so stupid?"

Annie's reception was enthusiastic. Dylan had known that he wouldn't feel fully comfortable in her presence; ironically, the warmer her gestures, the greater his unease.

"Never mind," he consoled himself, "I'll put all this behind me before long."

But things didn't work out that way. Dylan was surprised how much it bothered him to look at Annie, knowing he was hiding something from her. That she was ignorant of his indiscretion seemed to him to undermine their special relationship; they'd been wonderful together, but now, even in her warmest embraces he often felt distant and cold. Yet it still made no sense to tell; so he kept his thoughts to himself, still optimistic that soon his negative feelings would fade.

After ten days of malaise, however, Dylan began questioning his decision not to tell. True to his genuinely generous nature, he still thought it unfair to involve Annie, but was his unforeseen inner conflict trying to tell him something? As it happened, at about the same time a chat with Annie tilted the scales.

It took place in the kitchen before dinner on a Saturday. One window faced north-west, framing the church across the road. In the distance lay Burry Holm, a promontory at the north end of Rhossili Bay. Sunlight streamed through the window at an angle, highlighting a kitchen wall. Dylan sat at the table in T-shirt and shorts, mechanically massaging his hairline as he studied a book on the stars; he'd just put the children to bed. Annie approached from the hallway and sat opposite him. She wore a simple dress which she'd made; it was green with a pale red floral design. Her hair shone.

"Dylan? Are you all right?"

Naturally, he was on alert.

"Yes! Of course I am," and he chuckled, "Why d'you ask? Have I seemed different?"

"No, no! Well… not to me, except that you've been coming home from work later recently."

They smiled at each other, both enquiringly.

She continued, "Connie it is. She told me this afternoon that you don't seem to be as much fun these days. She seemed a bit sad and she threw me, to be honest."

Dylan was thrown, too, and unsure that he hadn't shown it.

"That's funny," he said, "She didn't say anything as she went to bed."

Brown, earnest eyes locked on very blue, but after a few innocuous observations Annie left for the sink, leaving Dylan to deal with a new, disturbing dimension to his predicament. He really thought he'd succeeded in putting a good face on things; a delusion obviously, and if his front could be penetrated by little Connie, how could Annie be far behind? Come to that, what lurked behind her look just then? He became convinced that soon she too would twig. At the thought of her probing, he actually chuckled to himself. He couldn't lie to her again; under her gaze, he would tell his story, and if then, why not now? A voluntary admission would certainly be seen in a better light.

"Just tell her! Get it off your chest! But why should I share my pain… Dylan, just tell her! Get your relationship back on track."

Only lightly did he rationalise his decision. He really did consider his indiscretion to be minor, and surely his firmness with that hussy in the end would carry weight. While Annie would be hurt, she wouldn't be hurt for long, and then he could be effortlessly warm to her again.

At the end of dinner the following day Annie was commenting on how settled the weather had been over the weekend.

"I'm sorry to interrupt you, Annie…"

She exaggerated her surprise.

"… but there's something I should have told you."

Annie smiled encouragingly.

"What is it, Dylan?"

Slowly, he told her of the hot tub and the show, his unpetty gesture, the failure of lift and lights, the woman's plea for comfort, her embrace and its disconcerting effect on him.

"I couldn't help it, Annie. Actually, it was embarrassing… and then she felt me."

Annie became animated.

"You're joking! She felt you?"

Dylan nodded seriously.

"It must have been nice," she said, "Why did you stop her?"

"That's the point, Annie. I didn't… well, not immediately anyway. I should have, I meant to, but I didn't."

Annie stared at him in disbelief. She then straightened and said, a shade angrily Dylan thought, "I can't believe you let her go on."

Dylan thought it best to remain silent.

"Did you…?" she asked.

It appeared that she couldn't say the word, but Dylan had

read her mind; he hoped the answer would provide him with redemption.

"No," firmly and with feigned indignation.

"Why not?"

"Because I stopped her after a while."

This seemed to make little impression, alas.

"So, is that all?"

Dylan nodded. By now, it seemed Annie had spent her emotion; her head and shoulders slumped and she exhaled. At this, Dylan felt a wave of warmth for her. For the first time since the incident he regarded her with feeling rather than awkwardness. This release brought him to life.

"Annie! Listen to me, please. I know I made a mess of things, but you must admit that everything ganged up on me."

Annie faced him again.

"I just wish you'd stopped her at the start; I'm shocked that you didn't. The whole thing strikes me as cruel, Dylan. We don't deserve this."

Dylan paused. Was he justified in feeling relieved? Still, it seemed important to press ahead and make his case.

"You know I'm not like that, don't you, Annie? For God's sake, I remember wishing you were with me in the hot tub."

"Dylan, I know! We live for each other… I know that, but I still don't understand why you didn't stop her right away?"

The same refrain.

"Annie, you've no idea how I've struggled… for ten days now. Do you think you'll be able to forgive me?"

"I don't know!" and she sighed as she shook her head, "I can't forgive you now. It's been a shock, you know."

As for encouragement, she hadn't thrown him much, but it moved him. Relief was at the root of this, of course, but so was his love for her, now in flower again after floundering for days.

Dylan rounded the table. For a quarter of an hour they sat in silence.

"She's obviously hurt," he thought, "but I can't believe it'll be for long," and then, "She's brilliant."

He kissed her hand gently, and then they cleared the dinner away.

"I think it would help if I could sleep on my own tonight, Dylan."

He wasn't surprised.

"Good night."

She looked subdued as she left. Not much of the aura of a goddess had she, but he worshipped her nevertheless.

# F I V E

I T'S NOT UNCOMMON in an unfamiliar bed to wake up to
an urgent feeling that something is wrong. In the gloom
around the room, recesses and objects are unrecognisable…
and disturbing, too, till suddenly all becomes clear. Annie awoke
early the next morning to a similar feeling, though she'd slept
in that bed a thousand times before. Something was amiss. It
weighed on her, and then the penny dropped.

"Why didn't he stop her before she got going?" she asked
herself angrily.

This thought she repeated several times.

Then, conceding perhaps that fate was at least partly to
blame, "Why me? Why us? We don't deserve this."

Occasionally, she even resented having been told. Stepping
out of bed, she fumbled with her dressing gown; it was light
blue with a ruffled collar, and she'd made it. It was only half past
five, but already light. She moved to the kitchen, drew back the
curtains to a grey day, and settled in her favourite armchair.

"Why didn't he stop her at the start? Perhaps I can't trust
him after all."

She'd planted a seed of doubt which to her horror began to
mushroom; she hadn't experienced this fearful feeling for years.
Testament to her seemingly complete recovery was that Dylan,
in arriving at his decision to tell, had not considered a possible
psychological setback for Annie. Just as in the past, a wave of
tension swept her stomach. As it settled there, she fought back;
instinctively, she clenched her fists and gritted her teeth.

"He may have slipped up, but what he did is not like Dylan
at all… and of course I trust him! Of course I do!"

This was thought with sufficient conviction to brush her doubt and fear aside. She still had to come to terms though with what had happened. Annie resettled in her chair.

Later, Dylan asked her, "Would you prefer that I didn't go to work today?"

"No, no! You go. Please!"

"Perhaps I should stay and talk to you."

"No, I'm not ready to talk yet, Dylan."

Before he left, he asked again.

"Are you sure you don't want me to stay?"

"Yes! Absolutely! Don't worry. I'll be fine," but she wasn't. While washing and dressing and feeding the children, she mostly went through the motions. It surprised her that the balance in her life could be upset to this degree, and by such an unlikely event.

"Don't think about it," was her self-reprimand, "Just get on with things."

Easier said than done, and at that moment it didn't help that the children were clinging to her, especially Connie who seemed determined to share in her mother's sadness.

"This is silly," she thought, "What I need is time to myself."

Five minutes later Annie walked away from the village towards her mother's house, a small pack on her back, Connor in pushchair, and Connie in hand. Peggy, still petite and pretty, greeted them excitedly.

"What a nice surprise." Annie smiled half-heartedly and asked, "Where's Daddy?"

"He's in the back in the garage; he's got a big job today."

No longer did Arthur drive buses; just a mechanic now, and a good one, in demand.

"Will you look after the children for a few hours, Mammy?"

Of course she would; she'd love to but, "Are you all right, Annie?"

"Yes, I'm fine. I've got a few things to sort out, that's all."

She knew this would set her mother wondering, but she had to say something. Peggy was tactful though; she left it at that, but she did look worried as Annie waved goodbye. Connie did too.

"Poor Connie," thought Annie, "She hasn't seen her mother upset very often."

Connor, however, seemed on tenterhooks, presumably keen to see his grandfather and Nia the dog.

On the cliff tops that lead to Worm's Head, low cloud cover portended rain. Still, Annie felt lighter: she was soothed by the sound of the waves below.

"Why didn't he stop her at the start?" and "It's not like him at all" was still the extent of her enquiry, though. For a moment she felt angry again that Dylan had confessed, but no, this was Dylan to the core, and she wouldn't want him any other way. Then something lovely happened. Approaching the spot where they'd picnicked a fortnight earlier, Annie was reminded vividly of how things used to be, and that she and Dylan were soulmates. The phrase "It's not like him at all," took on meaning, and so, in her thoughts, she took another step.

"If I'm certain it's not like him, then there had to be good reasons why he let her carry on."

But what good reasons could there be? She ran through the circumstances leading up to the incident, circumstances which Dylan had presented as extenuating. His defence became somewhat more persuasive. And yet, in the end, she hit the same brick wall.

"He should still have stopped her at the start. Why didn't he?"

Amidst these regurgitations, however, was a change for the better: a more generous view of Dylan's indiscretion had taken hold, so that when she met the children she was more attentive to them. It helped as well that her mother refrained from asking what was wrong.

That afternoon, soon after the children's nap, Annie's father turned up at the bungalow... in his working clothes. He was tall, even without his wife as a foil. His hair was thinning and greyish, and his piercing brown eyes exaggerated his slightly pointed nose.

"Hello, Connie! Did you have a nice nap, Connor?"

Connor beamed and nodded: he liked his granddad.

"No, I won't sit down, Annie. Look at me! My boots are a mess – it's wet out there. It's just that I drove the van back to Alex's, and I thought I'd stop by on the way home."

Annie sensed what was coming.

"You don't look well, Annie, and your mother said that you had a few things to sort out. So what's going on?"

Annie knew her mother would not have volunteered that information, and at the thought of the interrogation she may have gone through, Annie chose not to stall.

"I can't tell you, Daddy. It's private."

Why would she share Dylan's misdeed, when she wished sometimes that he hadn't shared it with her? Arthur smiled patronisingly and squared his shoulders.

"I know you're a bit down, Annie, but..."

"No, I mean it. I can't tell you."

She wished he wouldn't go on: she was upset enough as it was.

"Well, is it to do with Dylan?"

"Daddy! It's private."

He tensed; his brown eyes tightened. From experience

Annie could tell that he was debating whether to pout or to pester.

"Suit yourself. Mind you, I find your behaviour insulting… after everything I've done for you."

His tone had changed, and the children, standing next to him, noticed. In unison almost they gaped at him, and then at their mother. Meanwhile, Arthur didn't move, as if confident of a reaction. After a while Annie obliged.

"Look Daddy, I'm not just a little bit down, you know. I'm very upset, and you're only making matters worse by going on like this, so if you care for me one bit, then…"

Arthur turned and with no flourish made for the door as if all was well with the world.

"How typical," thought Annie, "and how childish."

Her father's prickliness was nothing new: she and her mother together had played along with it, had laughed it off usually, and more often than not had taken it in their stride. Today though, his indifference to her suffering had really hurt Annie… and angered her. The misgivings she'd initially harboured over not indulging him had been dismissed.

"He always expects to get his own way and he usually does… but not this time. I swear I'll never cave in on this. He'll be the last to be told of what happened."

Dylan came home earlier than usual.

"You're still angry at me, aren't you, Annie?"

"I don't know about being angry, Dylan, but I am disappointed."

Dylan shook his head. She told him of her father's visit, and concluded with, "His timing couldn't have been worse, but he didn't seem to care."

Dylan must have assumed that she, in getting this off her

chest, was reaching out to him, because he brightened. Annie had always joked that should Dylan and she need an avenue of reconciliation, she could always depend on her father.

"Dylan, play with the children, would you, while I make dinner. I think I'm ready to talk to you now, but let's do it after the children go to bed."

The rain had cleared and the sun was setting through cirrus clouds: it promised to be a gorgeous sunset. Annie felt on edge. She wasn't expecting a miracle from their chat, but by now she had hope which she feared might be dashed; a retrograde step would be hard to take.

"Why did you let her go on, Dylan? I wouldn't have thought that of you."

Dylan appeared ready with his reply.

"I don't know, Annie. The thing is that if I hadn't held the lift for her, nothing would have happened anyway; nor if the lift hadn't broken. If the lights hadn't gone out, I'd have stopped her there and then. If she hadn't said she was frightened, I'd have pushed her away, even in the dark. And nothing would have happened if she hadn't, shall we say, introduced herself to me earlier. She did excite me then, I admit, but I didn't want anything to do with her. I wanted you."

So far, the good reason that Annie had hoped for was not forthcoming, but neither was the backward step that she feared. If anything, Dylan's sincerity was hitting home.

"So why didn't I stop her? Given the way I am, and I was no different then, I should have reacted at the latest when her hand started moving down my stomach, but I didn't. I don't know why; I must have been drugged or something," and of course in a way he was. That moment in the lift when he should have stopped the woman may have coincided with the one when the experience had felt so good. So, he was not totally open, but still completely sincere when he said, "So, there I was in this situation. I hadn't looked for it and I didn't want it."

And on to this did Annie latch, in this she could believe. Perhaps the good reason she'd sought wasn't there after all; perhaps Dylan wasn't blameless. So, with no miracle at hand she would settle for time as her healer.

"Dylan," she said softly, "Let's not go over all that again. Just give me time, all right?"

He nodded... with relief, she noticed. The sun still hadn't set. That night she slept on her own again; it did appear, though, as if Dylan's prediction would come true.

"She'll be hurt but she won't be hurt for long."

# SIX

FOR THE SECOND day running, Annie awoke soon after dawn, and again to a sinking feeling. But then she suddenly remembered her conversation with Dylan the previous evening. She took several slow, deep breaths and reassumed the philosophical stance that she'd settled on: yes, time would be her healer.

"I think I have to accept that Dylan wasn't blameless, but I believe him when he says that he wasn't looking for it and that he didn't want it."

As dawn became sun-up which in turn became day, these thoughts, reassuring, were often in play, because she was not totally out of the woods yet; on the mend, though, and beginning to forgive, to the point that she thought with a chuckle, "I better prepare myself; he's bound to want to pamper me."

Annie had decided not to visit her mother that morning: she felt too angry with her father. Instead she would revisit their picnic spot. The weather was dry and calm and warmer than the day before. Mother and daughter wore white tights under matching pink dresses, and Connor's dungarees were appropriately blue – Annie was an excellent seamstress. As she left home with the children, the church caught her attention. Across the road from her bungalow, it was hard to miss; she couldn't help but notice it. This morning though her mind dwelt on it.

"It is impressive," she thought, "Weren't we lucky to be married there?"

Inevitably, vows of fidelity entered the picture, and happily, loyalty to Dylan rose on cue.

"I just can't think of him as unfaithful."

Whatever had happened… and how… that night, she was certain it was something Dylan would not have sought; so it must have been pushed on him. She was still surprised he hadn't resisted at the start but…

"It's that awful woman. It was her fault."

The effect of this assertion on Annie surprised her. Putting the blame squarely on that woman seemed to give her a lift; surely, it wasn't as simple as that? Then, as if authenticating the accused would lighten things further, she deliberately formed a picture of the woman. That she was plain was all that Dylan had said, but that wouldn't do for Annie: accelerating Dylan's absolution depended on that awful woman looking the part. Annie pictured a fleshy face, swarthy complexion, heavy features and a sensuous, asymmetric smile… reminiscent of an aging Elvis, but exaggerated and in female form.

"Come on, children," she said with an enthusiasm that caused Connie to cock her head, "let's go to our picnic spot."

Once home, Annie phoned her mother and asked her to come over while the children napped.

Peggy had kept her figure: it was petite and in harmony with her small, pretty face. Today, her hair was tied up in a loose bun; it was blonde and noticeably wavy. Her white, short-sleeved cotton top had a fairly low neckline. It was her nature to be understated, and yet, she couldn't help but look glamorous. Her golden retriever Nia sat at her feet and matched her colouring perfectly.

"Are you feeling better, Annie?"

Annie smiled, nodded, and added, "I suppose Daddy is still going on about me insulting him. He made me so angry; I'm not going to give in to him on this one."

Peggy lent forward and stroked Annie's hands sympathetically.

"It's just that he feels slighted when he doesn't get his own way, and then of course," and she threw her lovely head up and laughed, "he forces everyone to take sides. I didn't tell him what he wanted to hear, so now I'm in the doghouse too."

"Oh, Mammy, I'm so sorry," and she held her mother's face in her hands.

"Poof! I'll be fine, and you will be too. We can't let your father get us down."

After her mother left, there were a few occasions when Annie dwelt on the incident in the lift; each time, she invoked the woman's face, greasy and grotesque, to reaffirm Dylan's exoneration. He came home early again and greeted the children with gusto. Connie and Connor responded to his enthusiasm; it was as if they sensed a change in the air. Annie, subdued, smiled at their antics. Occasionally, Dylan glanced expectantly at her.

"Oh, just look at his expression."

Before she could react, she was distracted by Connie begging her father to take them for a walk through the village. He enquired of Annie, and she nodded. As soon as they left, Annie stood up smartly and moved a bottle of white wine from their little rack to the freezer; the timer was set at half an hour. They rarely drank during the week, but she felt the need to make a gesture of reconciliation with which she was comfortable. The bottle was opened and placed on the table with a couple of glasses just as the children arrived home. They rushed at her excitedly. She smiled warmly in response, her first warm smile – and dimple – for days. She looked up and there was Dylan. He glanced at the glasses and then gazed at her with his blue eyes and quirky smile; his relief was palpable. He looked as pleased as a little boy with a fish on his line; and to think that she was responsible for that. All at once, Annie felt pleased with her gesture, touched by her children's greeting and moved by Dylan's spontaneous response. She walked slowly into his embrace; they didn't kiss and nothing was said but, "Dylan, let's not mention that business any more."

As Annie had predicted, Dylan took to pampering: he poured the wine, sliced French bread and spiced it with pesto. They toasted, tasted, and then, "All right, Connie. You and I are going to make your dinner tonight so that Mammy can put her feet up."

"Goody," said Connie, and rolled her pink sleeves up precociously.

In turn, Annie offered Connor her lap. As they cuddled, she sipped her wine and was warmed by a feeling of normality. To think that only twelve hours earlier the future had appeared uncertain.

Later, over dinner, she and Dylan talked of every subject that came to mind, bar one. After washing up, she asked that they take a short walk around the church. It was still light, but the weather had changed: cloudy and very windy now. She leant on Dylan's arm; she felt woozy.

Annie and Dylan slept together that night, as the wind whistled and whined. She let him hug her, but she couldn't melt yet, and he was sensitive enough to leave it at that.

# SEVEN

THE NEXT MORNING, a Wednesday, the first thing to inconvenience Annie was the power. Once again she had awakened early, but to no sinking feeling.

"God! What a relief!"

She'd stolen out of bed to a blackbird's tune, melodic and mellifluous in the latter part of June. The future was looking promising again. In the kitchen, Annie had switched on the kettle and then settled in her favourite chair till she realised that the power was out.

She rang the electricity company which blamed the disruption on last night's gales. Dylan's reaction to the inconvenience reflected the household's more buoyant mood.

"I might as well go to work early, then. I know I'll get a cup of tea there."

The second thing to go wrong was that their car wouldn't start. Two phone calls were made immediately, one by Dylan to their friend Angus who also drove to Swansea daily, and the other by Annie to her mother. She described their predicament.

"I'm too upset with Daddy to talk to him, but…"

"Don't worry, Annie! Just leave it to me."

This was what she'd hoped her mother would say, and it even occurred to Annie that her father could use his visit as an opportunity to break the ice.

"Hoping against hope, I know, but still…"

The children were spruced and nourished. The third thing to bother her, but only slightly, was a visit from that woman's face. This time it was not invoked: it appeared in her mind without invitation.

"That's funny," and she frowned and shook her head, but the thought was soon dismissed as she became aware of her father at the door. He patted both Connie and Connor on the head. He appeared jovial enough but no eye contact with Annie was granted, not even as she handed him the keys to the car.

"So much for breaking the ice," she thought.

Hurt by her father again, she affirmed her determination not to yield to him. The children followed their grandfather to the garage. Before long the car was heard to come to life. It didn't surprise Annie that Connie was the one who bore the news.

"Granddad says he's got more work to do on the car, Mammy. He says he'll do it at home and it won't take long."

Annie nodded.

"Ask Connor to come now, will you, so that we can go for a walk."

Later, arriving home, she found the power reconnected and in the garage, their car; not washed though as per usual, Annie noticed.

The novel that Annie was reading had been neglected since Dylan's confession, but as the children napped she turned to it. After a while, that woman's face, greasy and grotesque, gatecrashed Annie's mind. Its occasional recurrence during the afternoon eventually annoyed her.

"I'll talk to Dylan about it," and at the thought even, she perked up. When told of this by Annie, Dylan seemed unperturbed and responded with empathy and encouragement.

"Even though you've got over the shock of what I told you, it could still have taken something out of you, Annie... made you vulnerable to these strange thoughts. But you'll be fine soon. You've handled things like this before. You're brave, Annie... I wish I was as brave as you."

Later, while sitting outside at the front of their bungalow on a bench, Dylan turned to face Annie.

"I feel so angry with myself about this business, Annie, but you've been brilliant. I knew you wouldn't be hurt for long."

Annie smiled coyly. She edged towards Dylan, sat on his knees, and laid her head on his shoulder.

Two days later, on the Friday, that vulnerability to which Dylan had referred was evident once again. Soon after Dylan had left for work Annie had a morbid thought.

"I know I'm handling this Marlborough business well, but… but what if I can't quite get over it in the end?"

Not only was this morbid but irrational. She was virtually over the upset already; Dylan had been forgiven.

"Well, what if I can't?"

Annie knew she'd be wise not to pursue this question; she knew she was asking for trouble.

"Come on!" she chided herself, "Square your shoulders and shake it off. Why should things change for the worse?"

But, for whatever reason, Annie was dwelling on doubt again; uncertainty persisted.

"Yes, what if I can't quite get over it? Dylan and I wouldn't be as close, would we… which is a worry because I know our relationship has helped to keep me grounded."

A wave of tension washed her stomach, as it had during the morning following Dylan's confession. It was as if that initial bout of doubt had kept its foot in the door and here it was again in a more sinister form. It was one thing to deal with the earlier tangible uncertainty to do with Dylan, but quite another when now it was intangible… contrived even… and had to do with herself. Still, she fought back, clenched her fists and gritted her teeth, just as she had as a girl. She made sure that she kept busy, as if a mind in motion would be a mind immune. Although attempts at reason failed, she managed to remain reasonably calm, all the while aware, however, that beyond a very fine line lay a slippery slope, and aware too that should she cross that line she would likely hurtle down that slope into her troubled teenage state of mind.

That evening she felt silly telling Dylan, but he treated her with the same understanding and respect as before. She was amazed at the ease with which he reassured her; together they reasoned without difficulty. They came to an obvious conclusion: due to Annie's strength and sense in dealing with Dylan's slip-up, they were already as close as they used to be.

"So what is there to worry about, Annie?"

"Nothing at all, Dylan," and she smiled as she held his hands, "But you'd think I'd be able to work these things out on my own."

The following morning, Annie felt energised, buoyed by her recovery the previous evening. It seemed that she and Dylan together could sort out any doubt which weighed on her. She couldn't explain her sudden fragility over the previous few days, but she was confident that she'd overcome it.

Even though it was a Saturday, Dylan had to go to work; he'd be home earlier than usual, though. Soon after he left, Annie and the children strolled through the village, Connor's hand in his mother's. Before long they settled in their favourite spot on the cliff top and plucked grass and tossed it to the wind. To her surprise, that awful face invaded her mind again, but this time accompanied by Dylan in his swimsuit. This was a disturbing development; Annie felt forced to react differently. She scrambled her thoughts and focused her mind on Burry Holm in the distance. Then, as a distraction, she talked incessantly to the children while hoping that Connie wouldn't think it odd.

Back home, as soon as she'd put the children to bed for their nap, the face reappeared, again with a swim-suited Dylan in tow. As before, it was rebuffed hurriedly, but she had little confidence that she could keep it at bay. This was terrible! She'd really thought this morning that she was back to normal, but here she was with another fight on her hands. She experienced a throwback, and that familiar wave of tension settled in her stomach. She stopped in front of a mirror.

"Come on, Annie! For God's sake, get a grip! It isn't as if you haven't had to deal with stuff like this before."

She braced herself and took a deep breath.

"Poof," she countered, "This awful thing will be quiet as soon as Dylan gets home."

To the contrary, visitations persisted. When Dylan was told of her predicament, he reacted less calmly this time. He was still sympathetic but clearly perturbed as well. He guided her away from the children; he countered her fears with passion.

"Tell me Annie… why did you invent this face in the first place? Because you thought it would help you get over your disappointment, right?"

He was holding Annie by the shoulders and with his gaze, begging her to accept his explanations.

"Well, you're already over it, Annie, and you and I are as close as ever. That face is irrelevant now."

Annie nodded pensively. She accepted his argument but it failed to dispel her concerns.

"Dylan, I told you what I was like as a girl… insecure most of the time and obsessing about the slightest thing. Well, I'm afraid I'm slipping back into that state; it's a huge disappointment, you know."

"Annie, you were alone then, bottling everything up, but you're with me now. You've seen how it helps to talk. The two situations are completely different."

Annie smiled and nodded; Dylan's points were hitting home. She accepted his embrace and whispered, "I'm sorry, Dylan, I really am. I wouldn't blame you if you got tired of all this."

Soon, she left to play with the children. Dylan opened the fridge and poured two glasses of wine.

It seemed Annie was at war with herself: a generous, confident side in conflict with an introspective, pessimistic one. For years, the former had not been challenged, but now for a week had been under threat. Why was that? The initial disappointment over Dylan's confession may indeed have upset her equanimity sufficiently to make her vulnerable to strange thoughts; it had softened her up, so to speak. The hurt inflicted by Dylan in tandem with the anger induced by her father may then have weakened her resolve further. In any case, it looked as if a chink in her composure had been prised open by a devil within, one who'd been dormant for years. For the moment, however, Dylan's persuasiveness in hand with the therapeutic properties of wine had buoyed her. Those forces at war within Annie were in delicate equilibrium; she was relatively calm going to bed.

The following day the floodgates opened; not even Dylan could contain the deluge. Throughout the morning, Annie was regularly visited by the face. What could she do but parry it and prepare to parry again. Gradually, this routine wore her down to the point that she became preoccupied with another morbid thought.

"Am I making this up," she asked herself, "or is this thing bothering me even more when I'm thinking about Dylan?"

This notion was not based on fact, but given Annie's temperament and fragile frame of mind, she couldn't shake the idea, and so it became self-fulfilling. From then on, each time she thought of her husband, the face popped into her mind on cue with a half-naked Dylan in tow. The consequences of this shift in her thought pattern were dire. Dylan, as a positive and supportive force in her life, was being neutralised.

That evening she went through the motions of describing her troubles to him, though she knew it would be to no avail. In his presence, the face stepped up its assault on her. The accompanying tension cramped her emotions. She felt a distance form between Dylan and herself... what a terrible feeling to see one's lifeline being severed. Nothing that Dylan said or did made a difference. Annie went to bed feeling low and alone.

The next few days saw no improvement in Annie. Dylan did his best to comfort her even though she'd told him it would be self-defeating.

"You see, Dylan, every time I think of you, this awful thing hounds me. It's as if it's out to destroy our relationship. I've fought and fought to change this... but I can't. It's a horrible feeling, and knowing what pain I'm causing you makes me feel even worse. I know I'm being unfair, but I can't help it."

At one point, a teary-eyed Annie knelt at his feet: she really wanted to reassure him of one thing.

"Dylan, this is not about you and what you did. You know that, don't you? I've got over that! I've forgiven you! This is all about me... about me, Dylan. You know what I went through as a girl. I'm back in that state, you see. So it's not your fault. Please believe me, Dylan!"

Annie was right: she'd regressed fully. To make matters worse, this had come out of the blue, had taken her completely by surprise. After seven years of composure and contentment, the disappointment involved was jarring. So on top of all else Annie was reeling from shock. Her comfort at that moment was her hope that soon she'd be able to regroup and manage this obsession as she had others as a girl.

Imagine her anguish when, on Wednesday afternoon, she found herself dreading Dylan's homecoming; dreading being with the one she loved? How bizarre was that? Yes, imagine her anguish and imagine too her shame. Annie was only too aware that her adversary was achieving what she perceived to be its goal; and aware of the same when she asked to sleep on her own that night. Dylan shook his head in puzzlement, but insisted that she take the bedroom.

By Friday evening, Annie felt beaten down; she was depressed.

The rapidity of Annie's deterioration had shocked Dylan too. He felt awful as well: to think that he was at least partly responsible for her abysmal condition.

"This is not about you and what you did, Dylan," had been Annie's line, but he knew better than that. Certainly Annie's flaws had been central to her breakdown, but his misdeed in Marlborough had set it all in motion. He still felt angry at himself for having been so stupid, but now foolish as well for having overlooked Annie's background when deciding whether or not to tell her.

"Looking back, it's obvious I should have kept it to myself. Poor Annie! And to think that a few days ago I thought I'd saved her from herself… what a joke that was!"

Guilt, profound sadness and frustration weighed on him.

"Should I talk to somebody and get some advice or give her time to get better? I think I'll just keep an eye on her for now."

He still believed though that Annie had grit; not many would have survived so well what she'd suffered as a teenager. Surely she wouldn't be down for long, and in the meantime he would do all he could for the children... and Annie too to the extent that she would let him.

# EIGHT

B Y TUESDAY ANNIE had emerged from her state of shock; she accepted her situation and tried to settle into a routine. She couldn't overcome her depression. Nor could she kick the face; in reaction, her only option in her mind was to distance herself from Dylan… amid profuse apologies. Where she could, however, she fought, and fight she did in the case of the children. She forced herself to dress them, play with them, feed them and take them on walks. Each was an enormous effort but she took encouragement from the resilience she'd shown under somewhat similar – though less debilitating – circumstances when she was a girl.

Naturally, Peggy was keen to console her daughter, but her attempts were rebuffed… here, too, amid apologies. When Dylan came home from work, she would retreat for a while: his presence was upsetting, and anyway she knew it was beneficial for Connie and Connor to spend some time with him alone. Though she'd really tried to be normal with the children, her suffering had inevitably filtered through. Occasionally, Connor's face betrayed such confusion that she couldn't stand it; she would hug him then and whisper, "I'm so sorry, Connor, but I'm doing the best I can."

In this way, each day in Annie's life limped miserably into the next. On Friday, she thought the unthinkable.

"If it's impossible for me to be nice to Dylan, maybe we should live apart for a while. Perhaps that horrible face would leave me alone then."

The thought was immediately dismissed as preposterous. She imagined the satisfaction felt by the devil within on being

handed such a plum on a plate. No! It was a stupid thought...
but one that would not go away. By Sunday she'd decided that
she had to speak to someone about it – but to whom?

She couldn't turn to Dylan: that would be unfair, and anyway
the face would be relentless. As for her father, he'd disqualified
himself. She was so angry with him; he'd be the last to be told
of her troubles. Her mother would have been perfect: wise,
understanding, and accessible, but she couldn't be asked to
keep her husband in the dark – he'd make her life unbearable.

"How upset will Mammy be," she wondered, "if I choose
someone else? She's not normally touchy but she might be about
this. I must explain it to her; then I'm sure she'll understand."

So, partly by default, Auntie Maggie became the one. She
too had Peggy's attributes and had always treated Annie as the
child she'd never had. As a result they were close, but not as
close as Auntie Maggie and her husband Trevor. To complicate
things, Trevor and Arthur were best friends on account of being
family, neighbours and colleagues for years driving buses.

"So I'll have to ask her not to tell Uncle Trevor. Will she
agree to that? Who else can I turn to, though?"

During the morning she phoned her aunt and arranged
for her to visit the following day while the children napped; it
would have been insensitive to meet while Dylan was around.

Auntie Maggie had aged well; too stocky to be thought of as
elegant but her posture remained impressive. She was aware
of Annie's troubles, and had assumed that the phone call had
been a cry for help. As she walked to her niece's at nap time she
felt confident that she could be of assistance.

Annie revealed that she felt she had to talk to someone
about her issues and that she, Auntie Maggie, had been chosen.
Auntie Maggie smiled self-consciously, only to be taken by

surprise immediately when Annie laid out the condition that Uncle Trevor had to be kept in the dark… and why. Put on the spot, Auntie Maggie wrote her dilemma all over her face; Annie reacted with a pained expression.

Suddenly, Auntie Maggie feared for her niece and felt shame over not committing herself; she was moved by a wave of love for the surrogate of a daughter she'd never had. At that moment she pledged herself to Annie, and without weighing the issues or considering the consequences, whispered, "I promise not to tell him, Annie… I promise."

Later, Annie told her story. Auntie Maggie was stunned by the complexities involved. Still, she conjured a couple of helpful suggestions despite her lack of relevant experience.

"Annie," she said in earnest, her receding brow furrowed, "Annie, don't rush a decision on Dylan. We'll talk about that later, all right? What I do want you to do though is take a bath before bed every night and take a long walk every day. It'll be a nice change and it'll get you out of yourself."

"But, Auntie Maggie, I don't have the chance."

"I'll take care of the children, Annie. I've been thinking that I could do with a change myself."

They agreed that Annie would go for a walk the following day. Then they parted, Auntie Maggie feeling more involved and connected than she'd felt for some time.

Trevor, nattily dressed, bespectacled and slim, met her in their front garden.

"How was Annie, Maggie?"

She felt she had no option but disclose her commitment to her niece… and her vow of confidentiality as well.

Later, over a pint at the pub, Trevor poured his heart out to Arthur. They were sitting by a window, but were oblivious to the view.

"I'm a big boy and all that. I don't need to know everything she does, but I must say this feels like a bit of a slap in the face."

From Arthur he'd sought sympathy, but was short-changed.

"Talk about kicking a man when he's down," was Arthur's response… short on sympathy, long on self-pity, "Why didn't she talk to me? Obviously, she's determined to humiliate me, and after all I've done for her."

Trevor was disappointed and countered with uncharacteristic punch.

"What are you all het up about? You don't have to live with your daughter, but I have to live with my wife," and as Trevor told his friend diplomatically that Annie was ill and could do with her father's support, Arthur left abruptly, his glass still half full. Yet, he greeted the other tipplers as if all was well in his world.

Oh, were he so at home with Peggy! Fortunately, she had been alerted by Annie who had explained with passion her reason for selecting Auntie Maggie. Peggy had been assured that under any other circumstance she would have been the automatic choice. As she was leaving, Annie had mumbled, "I love you, Mammy, I love you so much."

Peggy had been touched and was grateful for the alert. Still, Arthur's vehemence took her aback. He abruptly informed her that Annie and her family, as well as his sister Maggie, had been struck from his life, and that she, Peggy, better agree and fall into line… or else!

"Come on, Nia," he snapped at the dog, "Let's go to the garage."

These last two weeks had been trying for Dylan: worried by Annie's depression, frustrated with his inability to help her... and appalled by his role in the whole affair.

"There's no two ways about it. None of this would have happened if I hadn't screwed up in the lift."

Annie's condition worried him more with each day that passed. And of course it was hard to take her cold shoulder. He knew she had her reasons, but why couldn't she make the same effort with him that she had with the children?

"No, no! That's not fair! Considering what she must be going through, she's amazing with them. Connie even seems to understand how hard it must be for her mother."

During these two weeks, Dylan had often wondered whether to confer with Peggy, but each time he'd desisted, knowing how angry Annie felt towards her father. By the beginning of the third week, he'd become so concerned that he decided to consult their doctor, but that was put on hold when he was told by Annie that she'd confided in Auntie Maggie.

"Thank God for that," he thought, "although I'm not jumping for joy over Auntie Maggie being told about that woman in the lift!"

It was a small price to pay though for the huge relief he felt in knowing that another was in the picture, and not any old another. He admired Auntie Maggie: she had her feet on the ground and her medical background couldn't hurt. Her involvement was certain to expedite Annie's revival; her wisdom in concert with Annie's grit was to Dylan a recipe for recovery.

# NINE

THE CONFIDENTIAL NATURE of her commitment to Annie strained Auntie Maggie's relationship with Trevor, but there was sweet compensation: the satisfaction she gained from spending time with the children and walking with them whenever the weather was dry. Because she knew that Annie's daily trek took her to Burry Holm, Auntie Maggie thought it best to walk the children in the opposite direction – towards the cliff tops, where more often than not they were miraculously met by Peggy!

Now and then Connie would ask, "What's wrong with Mammy?"

"We don't know, darling, but she'll get better, don't worry. And remember what I said? She may get better sooner if we wish it. So let's close our eyes tightly and really, really wish."

It was noticeable that Connie had faith in this tactic, unlike Connor who quickly lost interest.

Despite Auntie Maggie's naturally optimistic mindset, by the Friday of her first week with Annie, she'd become discouraged. Annie was showing no improvement, and she couldn't drop the idea that perhaps she and Dylan should live apart for a while. As a result, Auntie Maggie was beginning to think that her niece would not rally without medical help. And yet, she was reluctant to rush down the professional path; surely Annie would soon snap out of the pattern of thought that shackled her.

Early that evening, Auntie Maggie had an opportunity to talk to Dylan alone in the village.

"How are you, Dylan?"

"Not special, I'm afraid. I'm sad for Annie… and worried."

"I know; I'm worried as well."

"And of course I'm upset that she won't talk to me much. I might even be angry with her if I wasn't so angry with myself. How could I have been so stupid? Not once but twice! I shouldn't have told her, Auntie Maggie."

"Dylan, c'mon now! I know what you're saying but in the end this is all about her… and she's obviously not well. To tell you the truth, Dylan, I've been wondering if she should see her doctor."

"Funny you should say that! I thought the same thing earlier in the week but dropped the idea when you got involved. By now, though, I just don't see her getting better on her own. You know something? If Annie wasn't a fighter, she'd be a total basket case by now."

"You're absolutely right. I know it's natural to think of anyone who's depressed as being a weak person, but if they keep on going… like Annie's doing… you could just as well argue the opposite. There's no doubt that Annie's got guts. Obviously, she's not able to stop these… what shall we call them… invasions of her mind, but we know that she's learnt to live with them in the past… just as she seems to have done with this one. It's not pretty I know… and it's hard on those of us around her… but the point is that it's not in Annie to give up. Coming back to the doctor, the only problem is that he's bound to recommend that she sees a psychiatrist. I don't know about you but in my time I've known some of them to go overboard. I would be afraid I may be throwing her to the wolves, if you know what I mean. And that's not to mention the stigma involved. Of course, Annie may well have to go down that road in the end, but I'm wondering if it's worth trying something else first."

Dylan seemed receptive.

"What is it, Auntie Maggie?"

She cleared her throat.

"Please don't take this personally, Dylan, but you and I both know that the face which she says is hounding her is somehow tied to you. What Annie says is that whenever she thinks about you, that awful face jumps in. She seems locked into that pattern, so I'm just wondering whether she's more likely to break out of it if she spends some time away from you... a fortnight, say?"

She deliberately omitted Annie's obsession with this idea.

"Perhaps a change is all she needs," continued Auntie Maggie, "to jolt her out of this mess she's in. What do you think, Dylan? Does it sound silly?"

Dylan didn't seem upset.

"I've thought of that, Auntie Maggie, but I didn't take it seriously. You think it might work?"

Auntie Maggie shrugged her shoulders, and Dylan continued.

"Personally I'd be surprised if it changes anything, but I'm willing to give it a go if you think it might help. Mind you, I wouldn't even think of postponing a visit to the doctor if I wasn't certain that Annie wouldn't harm herself. The children will be upset of course but I'll convince them that it won't be for long."

They agreed to the following: Dylan would broach the subject with Annie immediately and act as if it was his idea; if she accepted his suggestion and then there was no improvement in two weeks, Annie would be taken to see her doctor; better, however, not to mention the time limit to her, or to anyone else either. Auntie Maggie would break the news to Peggy.

On the Wednesday evening of the following week, Dylan idled in one of the myriad pubs in Mumbles: it was too chilly to sit outside. He'd moved into a hotel which overlooked the bay, and Auntie Maggie had agreed to drive the children there to be with him on Saturday. Over his pint and without being aware of his movements, he mechanically massaged his hairline. Of his emotions the most prominent was sadness: he was sad about his own circumstances, sad for the children and, above all, sad for Annie. His one comfort was the plan that he and Auntie Maggie had agreed on. Soon, one way or another, Annie's illness would be addressed. He'd be surprised, however, should Annie heal herself: much more likely was the alternative – a visit to her doctor, and he became uneasy at the thought of where that might lead. Yes, Dylan was sad. He found it hard to believe that his moment of madness had led to this: a domino effect which reminded him of the power of a flutter of a butterfly's wing. That a figurative pebble dropped in a hot tub in Marlborough had spawned a tsunami was mind-boggling. He hoped, but with little conviction, that this domino would be the last to fall.

Arthur was rampant; his face always appeared more pointed when his eyes were ablaze.

"I just knew at the time that that holiday in Tenby was a mistake. I told you, didn't I?"

Arthur was indulging his need to convince himself and others that whatever had been said or done by him – even seven years earlier – could never ever be wrong. Meanwhile Peggy, quiet and crestfallen, her blonde hair loosely tied in a ponytail, kneaded dough.

"And look at her now... no means of support. I suppose we'll be expected to help. Well, forget about it."

Peggy had no idea of Annie's arrangements, but she doubted that she would lack financial support. She then imagined her daughter's distress.

"I don't want to step on Auntie Maggie's toes or anything," she thought, "but I need to be involved. Even if Annie can't confide in me, I must be involved, even if it only means helping her put the children to bed."

No longer would she be discrete. Keeping the peace at home would take a back seat to the now pressing needs of Annie, Connie and Connor: there would likely be hell to pay.

# TEN

To Annie's surprise and relief, the face virtually disappeared; its mission accomplished, she thought with disgust. Yet, no respite was she given from her depression. One result of Annie's illness was a discomfort around people. Her ideal was to be totally unaware of the vitality and levity around her, a goal she came close to achieving on her walks by always wearing a hood. She had four of them, each an appendage of four green tops, designed for different conditions; so the changeable weather never deterred her.

The number of people on the beach at the Rhossili end of the bay varied with the time of day, the day of the week and the weather. At the Llangennydd end, however, over a mile and a half to the north, the wind and the tide carried more weight, as this was the spot that surfers preferred. On her walks, Annie's outward journey invariably took her along the beach: it was the shortest route to Burry Holm. At high tide, the promontory became an island, so Annie was sometimes denied access. When on it, however, with her back turned to her troubles, Annie's spirits were raised a notch. On the return journey, she sometimes left the beach opposite the surfers and took a higher route home. Once, on a fine day, she aimed higher still for the ridge of Rhossili Downs.

On these treks, hooded and insulated from her surroundings, Annie showed no interest in the surfers, but one of them in particular showed an obvious interest in her, and at her approach usually rested, and watched. Even from a distance, anyone other than Annie would have been struck by this surfer's closely cropped but dazzling blond hair.

It was a Tuesday, exactly a week after Dylan's departure. Annie had slept poorly. As a result, she was more down than usual that morning… and exhausted. In a daze, she fumbled and fiddled her way through her chores and forgot to have breakfast. So zombie-like was she that Auntie Maggie, arriving as usual at noon, expressed concern.

"What's the matter, Annie? You don't look well."

"Just tired, that's all."

Eventually, Annie prepared to leave on her walk.

"Aren't you overdressed in that fleece?"

"Well, it looks very overcast to me, Auntie Maggie."

In her state, Annie had misread the weather: overcast, it was true, but warm and close as well – typical thundery conditions. Once on the trail that led to the beach, she realised she was without water, but dismissed the thought as the green hood was flipped up. Annie felt strange from the start and suddenly so weak that her mind seemed detached from her body. It was eerie, but on she plodded wearily. At the Llangennydd entrance to the beach, many sat on the sand but the surfers were few. At that point Annie experienced a funny turn; presumably the heat within the hood and tiredness and hunger and thirst, together, had taken their toll. She became faint and, distressingly, lacked the energy to combat it; she felt a bit frightened. She sat on the sand, facing Burry Holm, and whispered, "Oh God! Why do I feel so shaky?"

She may have been calmer had she been aware of a head of blond hair idling on its board and watching her. At the moment when she decided she better turn for home, a distant thunderclap rumbled behind her, reviving a vivid and disconcerting memory. In her late teens, Annie and a girlfriend had been caught in a thunderstorm on Rhossili Downs. A lightning bolt struck so close that Annie had staggered, for it felt as if a hammer had hit her on the head. Nearby, her friend's face was ghost-like, completely drained of colour with a mouth that had shrunk into a little round hole. Since then, she'd been respectful of thunderstorms. Now, caught unawares by one, she became even more flustered.

"I can't go home; that's where the thunder is. I'll go to Burry Holm, then. But hang on! I'd be exposed out there, wouldn't I?"

In a mild panic now, she pushed herself to her feet and without thinking lurched towards the dunes and the path that led towards Llangennydd. There was more rumbling in the distance.

On her feet, still hooded and now slightly hunchbacked, Annie felt shockingly weak. As she shuffled slowly towards those who sat on the beach, she took quick, sharp, but shallow gasps of air. She wasn't thinking straight: otherwise in her state wouldn't she have appealed for help? She threaded through those who sat and skirted a squabble of herring gulls which were living up to their collective name by rowdily vying over a slice of bread. Later, she also chose not to approach the various bystanders in the car park. Her justification was jumbled, but in the mix were shame, pride and an assumption that no one would understand her issues anyway; but there was something else as well… an intangible force egging her on. To begin with she'd resented it, because she was so tired by now that she could happily have folded and fallen to the ground, even in the face of an approaching thunderstorm. Gradually, however, resentment had receded, and she'd come to accept that perhaps this was a force for good. Whatever it was that egged her on was certainly persistent.

"Left foot forward, followed by the right; Left foot forward…" it seemed to whisper. It took Annie a while to accept this phrase as a mantra, but as soon as she did, she felt less panicky. But oh, she was tired; so tired as to be oblivious to a change in the mantra's rhythm. It now moved in sync with her shuffling and her breathing; all three on the same steady beat. Without realising it, Annie became mesmerised by the rhythm… by the rhythm… by the rhythm. She was aware of nothing bar the rhythm… bar the rhythm… bar the rhythm. She fell into a trance-like state; nothing, not even the rumbling, would reach her now.

As she climbed a steeper segment of the road which skirted a caravan park, a dilapidated, black, low-slung car approached slowly from behind. It came alongside her cautiously, and slowed further. Annie glanced at it, and that's all. A surfboard balanced on the passenger seat; beyond it, eyeing her with concern, was the surfer, distinguished by a head of closely cropped, blond hair and, now in close up, by blue eyes and a fine light-brown complexion, flawless but for a mole on the left cheekbone. All this Annie saw at a glance, but it registered only in her subconscious. Annie, in her trance-like state, wouldn't remember a thing, not even the hurt on the surfer's face as Annie abruptly turned away. The car nosed ahead as distant thunder rumbled, but she was aware of nothing bar the rhythm; "Left food forward, followed by the right; left foot forward…" Approaching the top of the hill, she slumped to the ground; the mantra seemed to be losing its power. In her trance, she had neither a sense of how tired she was nor an understanding of the hallucinations that her exhaustion was about to bring on.

She struggled to her feet, and felt she'd have slumped again had she not imagined herself captivated by herring gulls swarming around her head. They'd appeared from nowhere, and continued to swirl and swoop and shriek as they encouraged her over the top of the hill and then down to the left towards Llangennydd. In this boisterous fashion, they held her attention till the mantra reasserted itself.

"Left foot forward, followed by the right; left foot forward…" and then the gulls vanished as suddenly as they'd appeared. As with the surfer in the car, this hallucination, and subsequent ones, would register only in her subconscious, she wouldn't remember a thing. Annie walked laboriously down the hill, past several houses and then up a gradient to the village proper. Twice more did the mantra lose her and, in her imagination, twice was she rescued by the squabble of herring gulls. On the second such occasion, she was approaching Llangennydd square, in full view of the tiny, triangular village green. She imagined the gulls egging her on towards the church, cajoling her into entering the lych-gate, and bullying her into lying on the floor just inside. Oh, Annie must have been so tired; wrapped in her dark green top and hood, she immediately fell asleep to the rhythm of the mantra which had reconnected with her.

"Left foot forward, followed by the right; left foot forward…"

# ELEVEN

ANNIE WAS AWAKENED by a booming thunderclap which had come right on the heels of the lightning fork which caused it. It was close. She shivered and roused herself; she noticed it was raining and then wondered where she was. What was she doing curled up on a concrete floor? She sat up, recognised the church, and then queried how she'd got there.

"Oh, yes! I remember now, stumbling from the beach and struggling through the car park; but what happened then?"

The last month had been so surreal that Annie wasn't particularly bothered by this conundrum. Another boom, then rumble; this one farther away.

"But why isn't the thunder making me nervous? I'm not complaining, but…"

The rain stopped, and the sun broke out to the south. Annie was captivated by a glorious rainbow which arched Llanmadog Hill.

"It's beautiful," she thought, "It's like a miracle," and that's when she realised that she hadn't felt depressed… not even then, when she'd made herself aware of it.

"Why do I feel different? There's something strange going on," Annie whispered, shaking her head, but before she could reflect on it, thoughts of Auntie Maggie intruded.

"Look what time it is! I should have been home by now. Auntie Maggie'll be worried stiff. I better hurry," and as she stood up she felt very weak and very thirsty.

"I can't walk all the way home feeling like this. What shall I do?" but without waiting for an answer she fumbled with the gate and stumbled into the road. On the far side was what once must simply have been a natural spring, whose water by now had been harnessed to flow from a pipe; still vigorously and enticingly, though. Annie knelt on the wet, slightly muddy, grass, flipped off her hood, reached forward, and with hands cupped, drank slowly. As she satisfied her thirst, the water bubbled; it seemed to be speaking to her. On it sunlight danced magically, and the whole experience began to play on Annie's mind. She sensed a presence which reached out and touched her; how exhilarating it was not to feel alone. Annie relaxed completely and experienced a beautiful peace; these sensations persisted as she gradually regained her strength. Eventually, they wound down; she stood up and glanced around. Given all that she'd been through recently, she could be forgiven perhaps for resenting the rainbow's disappearance; and forgiven certainly for not recognising the person in front of the pub up the hill. It was closed now, but at one of its less prominent alfresco tables sat the blond-headed surfer.

Her hood was down and the sun highlighted her hair as Annie set off for home via the route along which she assumed that she'd arrived. She reflected on the many unusual things she'd experienced; so unusual that soon they were no longer seen as a conundrum but as a series of miraculous events. How else to explain her serenity in the face of a storm and her delivery, at least for now, from depression… not to mention the presence that soothed her at the spring? She wondered if these events were in any way connected to her mysterious passage to the lych-gate.

"I suppose they might, but I don't know. One thing I ⟨ know though is that something special definitely happened.'

The more she reflected, the more she was persuaded ⟨ a supernatural hand must have been at work, a hand that touched her as she quenched her thirst.

"Hang on a minute," she countered, "Don't get carrie⟨

with this supernatural stuff! That might work in books and films, but..."

For some reason she was reminded of those two occasions on the cliff tops when as a teenager she'd imagined the wind to be her friend; she recalled her exhilaration at the time... but also the crushing let down that followed.

"So am I being set up for a disappointment again?"

A typical burst of doubt, which this time however failed to dent the feeling that she'd experienced something special.

"Obviously, I don't know what happened, exactly, but I know the effect it had on me. I felt as if I was blessed."

By now, Annie had passed the caravan park entrance and was walking on the path above the beach. The breeze was fresh, the sun was warm and the view was simply stunning; so why was she not jumping for joy? Well, she felt like it, naturally, but shied away. Surely when it came to miracles, immodesty was unseemly?

"And anyway, how many times have I felt better and got really excited, and then was crushed?"

How wise she was. Halfway home, whatever had earlier weighed on her threatened again and gradually tightened its grip... but she didn't fold as before; it seemed her experience at the spring had wrought a change for the better, had given her a shot of confidence. A resurgence of depression had been disconcerting, of course, and yet, Annie had a feeling that this time the effects would be more manageable.

"But am I sure about this? Am I sure enough to raise other people's hopes... the children's, for example? Hmm! I better not for now, just in case."

To Annie's surprise it was her mother who met her in the kitchen. Connie and Connor were playing on the floor; they glanced at their mother and waved.

"We were worried, Annie. Are you OK?"

"Yes, I am, but… what about Auntie Maggie? Is she all right?"

Something in Annie's tone had clearly caught Connie's attention. She left her toys and stood by her grandmother; she looked up at her mother expectantly.

"Yes, she's fine," said Peggy, "but she was worried about you too. She left a while ago because Trevor had come by to say that he fancied going out for a meal. As you know, Auntie Maggie does all she can to please him these days; so I agreed to come here early."

"I think I should phone her and tell her that I'm home safely."

As Annie turned towards the hall, Peggy said, "You seem different, Annie."

"Do I?" and that's all. She closed the kitchen door behind her.

"Hello! It's Annie. I'm sorry that I made you worry, but I couldn't let you know what was going on."

She listened, and then glancing towards the kitchen, spoke quietly, "Something special happened, Auntie Maggie. I can't say more now, and I know you can't come here tonight, but will you come over earlier than usual tomorrow?"

She seemed happy with the answer.

"I hope you enjoy your dinner with Uncle Trevor," and then more quietly still, "I want to tell you that I couldn't have managed without you."

Then, back in the kitchen, she said, "I'm very tired… and hungry too. If you don't mind, I'll take this apple and those bananas with me to my room."

Peggy and Connie looked at each other quizzically.

Annie slept well that night, but awoke to a sinking feeling; this time though she fought back. She remembered the hand that she was sure had touched her at the spring… a hand that would help her, perhaps? Admittedly, previous improvements in her mood had always reversed with a vengeance, but she had a feeling that this was different. She felt down, it was true, but now, thanks to that hand, she sensed a lighter shade of black at the far end of the tunnel. Later in the kitchen, Annie opened the curtains to another grey day, and as she gazed wistfully towards Burry Holm a dream came back to her. She dreamt a lot, but this one was last night's, and it was vivid. She was alone on a road, hooded and slightly hunchbacked. She stumbled, but was immediately encouraged and cajoled by a squabble of herring gulls. They swarmed and squawked around her head till she steadied herself, and then they vanished, only to reappear when she stumbled again. In this fashion they escorted her safely to a lych-gate and forced her to rest on the floor inside.

"Well!" thought Annie with a chuckle as she recognised the church in her dream as Llangennydd's, "I don't know what happened but that's one explanation, I suppose."

# TWELVE

ANNIE'S PHONE CALL had excited Auntie Maggie. "Something special has happened," Annie had said, and then, "I couldn't have managed without you."

In both content and tone, those comments were encouraging.

"What could have happened?" would dominate her thoughts. At dinner with Trevor her excitement had been apparent, intriguing him at first, but then resurrecting shades of resentment. As a result their evening was tarnished, and later, her night was disturbed. In the morning, for Trevor's sake, she'd been careful to contain herself, but as she walked to Annie's with umbrella in hand her excitement and optimism were given free rein again.

"How are you, Connie?" jauntily, "and you Connor?"

The children half smiled.

"Connie," said Annie, "Auntie Maggie and I are going to have a chat in the front garden. We'll be able to see each other through the window, so don't worry."

Once outside, Annie gave her aunt a hug. While in the embrace, Auntie Maggie, still excited, asked quietly, "What happened that was so special, Annie?"

Annie told her tale in detail. Auntie Maggie was heartened by the improvement in her niece's mood, and yet, the deeper she was drawn into the story, the greater her dismay.

"Oh, Annie," she thought, "It's lovely to see you coming back to life again, but I wonder if you're losing touch with reality. I know that's one way to ease the pain, but I can't let you do it, can I?"

In fairness to Auntie Maggie, she was aware that, put on the spot like this, she couldn't properly assess the situation; so, gingerly she went with her instinct to rein Annie in.

"Be gentle," she warned herself, "because you're groping in the dark."

Annie's tale was almost over.

"So you see, Auntie Maggie, I'm sure I was blessed at the spring. How do these things happen, I wonder? I didn't see anyone there but what I felt couldn't have been more real… or more special. What do you think of it all?"

Still relatively energised, Annie gazed at her aunt expectantly.

"And you really don't remember a thing about the way you got to the church?"

Auntie Maggie trod carefully; her aim to deflate a little and to hurt even less.

"No, not at all!"

"Well, you were very weak and terribly thirsty," said Auntie Maggie, "I can understand why your mind blanked out, as they say. And if it was anything like hypnosis, I've heard that people aren't quite the same for a while after they come to, which could explain why you weren't afraid…"

Annie looked disappointed, and then she interrupted.

"I think there's more to it than that, Auntie Maggie. But what about what happened at the spring?"

"Well, I don't know what to think about the hand that you say touched you except that you weren't yourself, were you? As for coming back to life, you were totally dehydrated and any old water would have revived you."

Annie nodded thoughtfully as she stared at her aunt. She then glanced at the children through the window before replying.

"I know what you're saying, Auntie Maggie. I have my doubts as well. After all, this sort of thing doesn't happen every day... but I keep on coming back to the way I felt at the spring: it was wonderful. So, despite what you say, it's hard for me not to believe that something special happened there."

Auntie Maggie thought it best to back off. She lowered her head, nodded, and whispered, "All right."

"The other thing is I felt as if someone was taking care of me, someone who might help me to get better, perhaps."

This struck a chord with Auntie Maggie. It was her very role that was being paralleled by whomever it was that Annie had divined, and seemingly successfully, whereas she for weeks had failed. She wondered if her instinctively sceptical view was awry.

"I'm beginning to feel I need time to think," was her thought, "so I wish Annie would change the subject," and in a way she did.

"By the way, is there anything special about the church?"

On safer ground now, Auntie Maggie replied without hesitation, "Well, it is the largest in Gower and the only one with a lych-gate," and attempting to retain the initiative, she rambled on, "They say it was founded by St Cennydd more than fourteen hundred years ago. If it's something special you're after, you should hear his story... but you've heard it before, I'm sure."

"No, I don't think so."

"It wouldn't take me long to..."

"No, no, no, no! It's time I went for my walk, Auntie Maggie. I'm going to go back to the church today."

Auntie Maggie waved at the children as her niece turned and approached the back door. Later, Annie left, wearing a green top without a hood. Interesting, Auntie Maggie thought; another point to ponder whenever she had time to think.

Annie was naturally disappointed with Auntie Maggie's reaction. Others, faced with a similar challenge, might have blown it away with bluster, but she respected her aunt and was sensitive to her comments. There was another thing too: she couldn't dismiss Auntie Maggie, for without her aunt's support, she could see that it might become harder to keep on believing in her special experience.

Annie reacted to these concerns by dampening her expectations. As she walked above the beach, she decided that she'd be wise today to wish for very little. A sign would suffice: any sign which confirmed that her experience at the spring and the lych-gate had not been misconstrued. As she contemplated disappointment, her habitual sinking feeling took hold.

By now she was beyond the entrance to the caravan park, and the stretch of road ahead reminded her of last night's dream wherein she was escorted to the lych-gate by a squabble of herring gulls.

"Not a gull to be seen today," she thought sardonically. Yet, on the back of a burst of energy, she enthused, "But what if they did turn up? Yes… what if they did? Now that would be a sign, all right," and she brightened, till concern with what lay ahead consumed her.

As she approached the village of Llangennydd, consecutive sightings of the green, the church, the lych-gate and the spring lifted her mood slightly, but that's all; not even the bubbling had much effect. Her expectations had been dampened, but still, this was disappointing. She rushed to reassure herself.

"Now remember, Annie, you're not expecting much to

happen. You're just looking for a sign," and she almost missed it as the fear of failure weighed on her. She'd half opened the gate to the churchyard before she noticed the four scenes carved on it. In the one on the left a baby in a basket floated on choppy water, escorted it seemed by...

"Good God! I can't believe it! So I was right all along! From the moment I woke up here yesterday I knew there was something special going on."

Despite her excitement, Annie forced herself to justify the significance of the carving.

"So yesterday, I found myself at this church, but I've no idea how I got here. All I know is that while I was here I felt I was in someone's presence and was blessed. Then, last night I dreamt that I was ushered to this special place by herring gulls. Far-fetched, of course, but now at this very same spot I find a picture of a helpless baby in a basket, also in the care of birds... which look very much like gulls to me. I really wasn't expecting much today, but..."

This was an amazing coincidence, to say the least, but to Annie it meant more than that: her mysterious passage to the lych-gate, her inspiration there and at the spring, and her dream featuring gulls had all been cloaked in mysticism. Now, at this special place, an essential ingredient of those events was mirrored by a carving that couldn't be more real. In Annie's mind it lent credence to her mystical experiences.

"Even Auntie Maggie will be convinced by this; even she will have to agree that it looks as if a spirit is offering me support."

Annie had no idea what the picture represented, but she knew it was a sign, all right. In wonder, she touched it... all over. Then, after glancing at the other carvings, she passed through the gate and sat on the bench near where she'd slept the day before, absolutely certain now that she'd not overplayed her experience at the spring.

While Annie sat on the narrow bench, her excitement gave way to a peaceful feeling. It was nowhere near as intense as the beautiful peace that had embraced her at the spring, but it was noticeable all the same. It reinforced her conviction, and in her mind it seemed to connect her to the spirit, to the hand that had touched her a day earlier. Annie straightened on the bench. It made no sense to leave this magical place, but out of fairness to Auntie Maggie she must; and anyway, Annie couldn't wait to fill her in. Before setting off, she drank of the spring, its surrounds less muddy than yesterday. On the way home, threats from whatever it was that had weighed on her were easily rebuffed; she just knew that someone or something cared for her and had given her strength. She no longer walked alone... what a wonderfully secure feeling that was! So confident was she of a change for the better that now, unlike yesterday, she saw no reason why the children should not be made aware of it too.

"Annie seems locked into a pattern. Perhaps a change is all she needs to snap out of it."

This had been Auntie Maggie's justification for suggesting that Dylan leave home for a while. The move had succeeded with respect to the face, but had failed to break another pattern... Annie's depression; "Each day in Annie's life limped miserably into the next."

Annie had often tried to come to grips with her depression. Each time it had taken an enormous effort, and now and then she had managed to raise her spirits, but there was an inevitability to the relentless extinguishing that followed. After a while, she'd given up trying; hopelessness set in!

Whatever had happened yesterday to Annie at the spring, it

had given her a shot of confidence… and, just as importantly, hope. Her depression had then returned, but as we read in the previous chapter, "Annie had a feeling that this time the effects would be more manageable." She had still felt down, "But she had sensed a lighter shade of black at the far end of the tunnel." The pattern of her depression had been dented.

Today, hope had been bolstered by conviction and, as we saw, "She became absolutely certain that she hadn't overplayed her experience at the spring; she was sure a spirit had taken her under its wing and had given her strength."

Annie's confidence had been restored, in large part because, "She knew she no longer walked alone." On the way home, "Threats from whatever it was that had weighed on her were rebuffed."

The pattern of her depression had been broken.

Annie had arrived home from Llangennydd.

"Come here, Connie… and you, Connor," with her dimple in action, endearing again.

Though Connor's response was cautious, Connie's was immediate; after all, she'd already sensed a change in the air. Her face was filled with a smile, his coated with bemusement. He hung back, prompting his sister to take his hand and walk him into his mother's embrace. Annie was clearly moved by her son's confusion and her daughter's selflessness. As for Auntie Maggie, she just shook her head in wonder.

"Something else must have happened," she thought, "I wonder what it was this time. In any case, I'm thankful I had time to go over what Annie told me this morning."

She'd thought while the children had slept, and had succeeded in putting Annie's experience at the spring in perspective; whatever had happened there, Auntie Maggie had come round to the opinion that it was harmless enough, especially in the context of the healing it had induced. Had she stuck with her scepticism, how mean and miserable she'd have felt at this moment, an intruder at this trough of joy. As it was, Annie's elation infected her, just as her anguish had done for weeks.

"I've no idea what happened today, but I'm so happy for Annie; and look at the children. Just think of what they've been through."

What struck Auntie Maggie as remarkable was that Annie's demeanour seemed normal. For one who'd obviously flirted with the fantastic, she was perfectly at ease with herself. Perhaps then, as Annie's confidante, she should encourage her spiritual side, while not forgetting to rein her in, of course, should fantasy threaten to get out of hand. Auntie Maggie's ruminations were interrupted by, "I know you children are excited, but I'd like you to play on your own for a while, because I want to talk to Auntie Maggie."

"But we like to talk to her too," from Connie.

"I know that, darling, but I want you to give us a few minutes, all right?"

Reluctantly they turned to their toys on the kitchen floor. Auntie Maggie was hastily led to the hallway where an animated Annie described an amazing picture on the lych-gate and a dream that she hadn't thought of mentioning earlier.

"I suppose you know all about that carving," but before Auntie Maggie could comment, Annie continued excitedly, "You see, all I hoped for was a sign; confirmation, really, that I wasn't making more of all this than I should. Well, that scene on the gate was some sign, don't you think? And what's more, I've felt my old self ever since."

Auntie Maggie was smiling and shaking her head again.

She couldn't help but be impressed, and on the face of it there was no call to play down these two events; how could their conjunction be construed as sinister?

"Anyway, I've already decided that I should encourage her spiritual side," she thought, "because surely my most important duty is to keep her happy."

Then, out loud, "The four carvings, Annie, are vignettes of…"

Auntie Maggie stopped mid-sentence, suddenly struck by unease over where this storyline might lead them; too late though – Annie was engaged.

"What were you going to say, Auntie Maggie?"

What could she do? She had to respond.

"Those carvings are vignettes of the life of St Cennydd."

"You mean the baby in the basket is St Cennydd?"

"Yes."

"Really!" and Annie's mood changed; she became noticeably contemplative.

"I think I'd like to hear St Cennydd's story after all."

"But, Annie, it was only this morning that you said you didn't care to," was Auntie Maggie's attempt at deflection.

"I've changed my mind, Auntie Maggie."

Annie's tone was firm. Meanwhile, Auntie Maggie's unease had taken shape; she now knew exactly how Annie would react to the saint's story.

"Hmmm!" she thought, "I'm not sure if I'll be comfortable with this outcome."

Still, she had no choice but to tell St Cennydd's story, one which had been told and handed down for centuries and in the process had embedded itself in local folklore.

# THIRTEEN

THEY HAD MOVED to the lounge; Annie, still obviously preoccupied, settled on the couch with a happy youngster in each arm. Opposite them sat Auntie Maggie in a chair, leafing through a book that she'd retrieved from home: she was determined to narrate with poise, despite her reservations.

"Once upon a time, around 525 AD to be more exact, a beautiful young princess in Brittany was made pregnant by her father Dihocus. Months later, her father was summoned to attend King Arthur's court at Loughor, not far to the north of Rhossili. He took his daughter with him, and while there she gave birth to a son who unfortunately was born a cripple, with the calf of one leg attached to its thigh. Out of shame, Dihocus determined to dispose of his son, but before he could do so the baby was christened and named Cennydd. On his father's orders, the baby was placed in a Moses-like wicker cradle and set into the river Lliw; it was then carried by the current to the river Loughor, and swept out to sea. Soon, a storm moved in, but the cradle remained upright and was ushered by a swarm of gulls towards Worm's Head. Once there, the birds carried Cennydd to the safety of a hollow in the rocks."

Annie became exuberant. She sat up, began to interrupt, but thought better of it. She settled back on the couch to Connie's curious glances.

"The gulls plucked feathers from their breasts to make a bed for little Cennydd, and with their wings spread wide, sheltered him from the weather and the wind. When he was nine days old an angel presented him with a bell in the shape of a breast. Each day a doe filled it with her milk; in this way was Cennydd fed.

Interestingly, as he grew, his clothes grew with him as bark does on a tree. The angel visited him regularly and instructed him in Christian teaching, and informed him, when he was eighteen, that the time had come to leave Worm's Head. At this point the story becomes less definitive. Some would have us believe that Cennydd travelled the short distance to Burry Holm and established his hermitage there. Others contend that the site of the present Llangennydd church is the spot that he chose. Regardless, he found the journey taxing. He stopped twenty-four times, and at each halt a spring appeared miraculously so that he could quench his thirst."

Annie sat up again. Her lips were moving; obviously she was dying to say something, but she restrained herself. Connie felt no such restraint.

"Are the springs still there, Auntie Maggie?"

"Well, there's definitely one across the road from the church in Llangennydd, which makes me think that Cennydd's hermitage was set up there. Why would he, as lame as he was, go so far out of his way if he was aiming for Burry Holm? And though there probably was a settlement on the promontory as well, we actually know that at Llangennydd there's been a monastery, and then a church, for a thousand years and more. Anyway, back to the story. Cennydd became famous around the region. His bell was known as the Titty Bell, and represented his magic wand. It is reputed that with its help stolen goods were recovered, thieves converted to Christianity and at one time an army of soldiers destroyed. With one touch of his bell, Cennydd would skim across Carmarthen Bay to visit his friend David in Pembrokeshire. And yet, despite his extraordinary powers, Cennydd remained a modest and kindly man."

"Is he still alive, Auntie Maggie?"

"No, Connie, I'm sorry. He…"

"If he was good at magic, wouldn't he live forever?"

"I don't know about that, Connie. The story goes that he moved back to Brittany, and that's where he died. These days we know him as St Cennydd."

Connie appeared satisfied and settled back on the couch, while Connor snuggled up to his mother. Meanwhile, Auntie Maggie became aware of Annie gazing at her with a mixture of enquiry and excitement; her smile and furrowed brow in conjunction.

"She can't wait to get things off her chest," Auntie Maggie thought, "All I hope is that I won't be sorry that I told this story."

The silence was broken by the opening and shutting of the door of the back porch.

"Is anyone there?"

"We're in the lounge, Mammy. Come in!" from Annie brightly.

The pretty little face that appeared was coated in confusion. Peggy, no doubt, had been taken aback by Annie's sociability.

"What's happening?"

"Mammy's feeling better, Grandma," beamed Connie.

"Are you?" mimed Peggy.

Annie smiled, and with the dimple in the ascendant, nodded. Then she rose, ran towards her mother, and hugged her… and there they stood, crying. Despite her disquiet, Auntie Maggie was moved, and on the verge of tears herself. She allowed herself a brief congratulation on having persisted in her role as Annie's confidante. It hadn't been easy, but this emotional reunion made it all worthwhile.

"Just look at the two of them," she thought.

In a while, still in embrace, Annie whispered, "Thanks for being so nice about me choosing Auntie Maggie. I'm not sure

I'd have been as understanding as you. Anyway, I love you all the more for it, Mammy" and then, so that all could hear, "I'd like to talk to Auntie Maggie for a minute. Do you mind if I walk her home?"

After Peggy shook her head, Annie continued, "Just a few minutes, that's all. Come on, Auntie Maggie," and turning to the children, "I won't be long, I promise."

Once outside, Annie couldn't contain herself.

"The coincidences are overwhelming, Auntie Maggie."

She was very excited; the brown in her eyes and her hair was alive. She declared what Auntie Maggie had known she would.

"It's obvious now, isn't it, that St Cennydd is the one taking care of me and that he's the one who's given me the strength to get well again?"

It was only half an hour earlier that Auntie Maggie had defined her primary role to be the guardian of her niece's recovery. Yet, Annie's confident identification with the saint had so perturbed Auntie Maggie that an instinct to pour cold water almost got the better of her. Just in time, she gagged her gut feeling and simply said, with a measure of empathy even, "How can that be, Annie?"

"Oh come on now, Auntie Maggie," and she took her auntie's arm, "I didn't mean to say that my healer is St Cennydd himself – I meant his spirit in some form. Mind you, if he's good at magic," and here she laughed, "he might still be alive, of course."

Annie disengaged her arm, and aglow with enthusiasm, turned to face her aunt.

"Auntie Maggie, listen. Just think of these things I have in common with St Cennydd: I dreamt I was cared for by gulls… and so was he; I experienced something special at a spring which he created and drank from himself; also, you say that he founded his hermitage at one of two spots. Both of those places are special to me. You know that I found some relief on Burry Holm, and you know as well that my experiences at the church have helped me overcome my depression. These connections are convincing, don't you think?"

Annie Maggie smiled, and nodded: her priorities had been re-established, largely on account of having just pictured Annie in the lounge a few minutes earlier with the children content on the couch and with mother midst tears of joy. How could anyone presume to hamper such happiness? And anyway, there was no sign of Annie losing touch with reality. Despite her identification with St Cennydd, she was behaving remarkably normally.

"I know all this is hard to believe, Auntie Maggie," Annie continued, "but don't the facts speak for themselves? Oh, there's Uncle Trevor," and she waved at him gaily, "I better go now before I get soaked… look at those clouds moving in. And, anyway, they're waiting for me at home, aren't they?"

Further proof, to Auntie Maggie's relief, that her niece had her feet firmly on the ground. Annie's reward for unwittingly reassuring was an exaggerated and lingering embrace from an aunt… who wondered whether to phone Dylan.

"No! I'll wait until we take the children on Saturday; we'll tell Dylan then. I better give Annie a few more days to show that she's really better."

"What made you better, Annie?"

On her short walk home Annie had crafted a response to her mother's inevitable question. With an apologetic expression she hugged her again. In the embrace, she whispered, "What I've been through is impossible to explain, Mammy, and I'm afraid that my healing is more complicated still. I'm so sorry but I'd rather not say any more yet. Do you think that you can just accept that I'm better and just be happy for me, and spend as much time as you can with the three of us?"

Her mother tightened her embrace; that was answer enough.

The next several hours were spent making up for lost time. The children in particular revelled in this sudden relief from tension. A few times, that familiar weight which had dogged Annie for a month appeared from nowhere. Each time it was deflected handily, and it left no unease. Annie knew that no longer did she walk alone. Eventually, Peggy rose to leave.

"Even though I'm better, Mammy, we'd still like you to come here every evening."

Peggy's face reflected gratitude.

"I know how uncomfortable it must be for you at home, but surely Daddy will back off now when you tell him that I'm better?"

Peggy shook her head, her face petite, her expression intense.

"He made me very angry," continued Annie, "and I still feel it, but I suppose I could make myself apologise."

"That won't help one bit, Annie. He won't be happy till you open up to him, till you show him some respect, as he keeps on saying."

"But I can't possibly…" with her voice raised.

"I know, darling, I know. I'm with you. He's got away with his game for far too long."

Another embrace ensued. To their delight, this one was joined by the children.

"So long, Mammy! We'll see you tomorrow, then."

Later that evening, Annie read the children to sleep. Connor had wanted her to sit on his bed, and Connie had smiled her agreement; she obviously gained pleasure from pleasing her brother. At that moment, Annie had felt proud and so lucky; once again she was capable of showering her children with uninhibited maternal love. Soon after, she lounged in her favourite chair in the kitchen, sipping a glass of wine, and became aware of a persistent, rapid dripping outside the kitchen door.

"Oh, it's that same old hole in the gutter again; it must be raining hard though."

At that moment she realised that she hadn't noticed the dripping recently, and it wasn't as if it hadn't rained. The truth was that for a month she'd been completely caught up in herself, largely oblivious to her surroundings; now though, no parrying, no stewing, just noticing, hearing and thinking. What a wonderful feeling it was, and what a relief as well.

A photograph on the wall of the children hugging Dylan caught her eye; her feelings for him at that moment belied the turmoil and hurt of the last month.

"I love him so much," and that's when she felt the face attempting to kick in, but to her relief, it failed. With no effort on Annie's part, her adversary evaporated and with it Annie's residual doubts; at that moment, she knew she was whole again.

"Dylan's been so good to me," and she warmed to the prospect of reconciliation, but shouldn't she wait a week or so, to get her feet on the ground, so to speak, and rebuild her relationship with the children first?

"Perhaps Auntie Maggie should take them to Dylan on Saturday. He'll be disappointed, of course."

She would write him a letter, pledging her love, but

explaining that its consummation may be all the better after a short period of rehabilitation.

Annie refilled her glass, resettled in her chair, and thought. She couldn't get over the joy she felt each time she became aware that her mind was again as free as a bird.

"I suppose Auntie Maggie will tell Dylan what happened to me. What will he think? He's bound to be sceptical, isn't he? Auntie Maggie was too but, fair play, she is behind me now. The thing is I'm convinced that something special happened to me, but I can't explain it to anyone. I can't even explain it to myself. I just accept it, that's all."

Once again, after a month's hiatus, Annie's mind was grounded in a certainty, one on which she could depend. Earlier, it had been her relationship with Dylan… now instead, it was a strength that, as she saw it, emanated from St Cennydd through the medium of his spirit. Still lounging in the kitchen, she thought with welling affection of her mother and Auntie Maggie.

"Poor Mammy, though, tied to my daunting father. He did upset me," but now that she was joyful and generous again, her estrangement from him seemed childish. She resolved to apologise, despite her mother's pessimism on that score. She would go out of her way to be nice to him, beg him to move on. This she would do tomorrow.

Annie rose to close the curtains and caught herself in a mirror. She'd almost forgotten what she looked like.

"And look at my hair!"

It hadn't been trimmed for weeks. Annie analysed her reflection; she went deep within herself, and felt grateful. She wondered if her father looked at himself in this way, and if so, did he like what he saw? It was remarkable really how people contrived to live with themselves.

When in bed, she wondered why she'd been the one that St Cennydd had chosen to heal.

"Why did he choose me of all people? He must have a reason; he must have a purpose in mind."

She fell asleep content with the thought that Auntie Maggie was solidly behind her. During the night she woke up from a dream, recalling it in detail. It surprised her in two ways. First, it reprised the previous night's dream. As before, she was alone on a road, hooded and slightly hunchbacked, but before she arrived at the spot where she'd stumbled in the earlier dream, a black car nosed past her. Over the passenger seat lay a surfboard. The driver had closely cropped, dazzling blond hair, blue eyes and a fine light brown complexion, marred only by a mole on the left cheekbone. The second surprise was that she was sure that she'd never seen this person before in her life. She'd thought that she dreamt only of people she knew, and this departure puzzled her. She lay awake for a while.

Peggy was furious: she'd known that Annie would fail in appeasing her father. Still, Arthur's response had been inhumane. As she harangued him she seemed to grow in stature.

"I can't believe you wouldn't talk to Annie… and after all that she's been through. You really are an ogre sometimes."

Arthur remained calm.

"That's the whole point, isn't it? You say she's been through the ringer, but she hasn't turned to me at all. As for not talking to her, she knows the rules; she's not welcome in this house until she shows respect. An apology is all well and good, but it doesn't do the trick, I'm afraid."

Peggy wouldn't let up.

"Look! The point is that in everyone's life," and she

emphasised this phrase, "in everyone's life there is something so personal that it can't be talked about."

"If you're referring to Annie," calmly again, "her issues weren't so personal that she couldn't talk to Maggie about them."

Caught on the back foot, Peggy became angrier still.

"Because Maggie is sympathetic, that's why, sympathetic in a way that you've rarely been. You don't deserve to know what's going on in Annie's life."

As she turned to leave the kitchen, Arthur, menacingly she thought, riposted, "Who's to say I don't deserve to know, but I will find out, you'll see."

Such disharmony, especially with her husband, always saddened Peggy, but "Goodness me, he brings it upon himself."


"Mammy's feeling better now," was the first thing Connie said.

Dylan seemed confused, though it was clear that Connor's face was reflecting a change for the better as well. Naturally, Auntie Maggie's opinion was sought.

"Is she?" Dylan asked.

Auntie Maggie nodded.

"I must admit I'm surprised."

"And she's been good for days. I didn't phone you because I wanted to be sure first."

At last, confusion gave way to a quirky smile.

"What happened, d'you think?"

At the first opportunity, Auntie Maggie told him in detail. Dylan shook his head and exhaled.

"This is all a bit strange, Auntie Maggie."

"I know, Dylan, I know. I don't understand it any more than you, but it's working; you should see her. It's hard for me to accept her convictions, but I'm still supporting her. What she tells me is that her special experience, as she calls it, has given her strength, given her confidence. She's convinced that St Cennydd's spirit is looking after her, so she's not afraid of that devil within anymore. How can anyone knock that?"

"Can this last, d'you think?"

"She's been like this for days, and seeing her so happy, I'm not even thinking about that for the moment."

His smile returned, broader now, but then suddenly serious, he asked, "Why didn't she come with you today?"

He was handed Annie's letter. After reading it he said, "And this is a bit strange as well. Here! Read it! Tell me what you think."

She took her time before responding.

"Dylan, I don't think it's odd. She's been through hell, so even getting better is a huge adjustment. I'm not surprised that she feels she needs time."

Dylan nodded in apparent agreement.

"Should I phone her, d'you think?"

"I'd leave it to her. Let her make the first move."

"All right."

His smile returned; he started laughing to himself and hugged the children in turn. Then he asked, "Are you certain she's better, Auntie Maggie?"

"Yes, Dylan, she's happy; she's just as she was before. Ask Connie! Now, I've already mentioned my reservations to you, but you should see her! Despite her unusual convictions, she behaves perfectly normally."

"So you're sure of this?"

"What's on your mind, Dylan?"

"Well, my company asked me to go to Edinburgh... to a conference that starts on Monday, but I couldn't agree to go with Annie in the state she was in; but if you promise me she's better and now she tells me she'd like some time on her own, I'm wondering if I should go after all."

"Oh, Dylan, you should. You should! I'm sure Annie will be fine. What will you gain by hanging around here?"

"But it doesn't feel right, somehow."

"Dylan, do it! You won't be gone for long anyway, will you?"

"Well, I'd leave on the train tomorrow and be back Wednesday night. If you really think it's all right for me to go, I'll book a room. I'll have the name of the hotel and phone number for you when you pick up the children this afternoon. It sounds as if the programme will be pretty intense, so I'll probably not phone you unless there's a change in my plans."

Soon they made their goodbyes, and then from Dylan, "Tell Annie I'm so happy for her… and that I can't wait!"

# FOURTEEN

AUNTIE MAGGIE HAD admitted to Dylan that it was hard for her to accept Annie's interpretation of her recent experiences. Despite her commitment to be the guardian of Annie's recovery she couldn't completely bury her concern over her niece's unusual convictions. Imagine a cynic's interpretation of this: "In the wake of Annie's recovery, in the aftermath of natural expressions of joy, don't you now, Auntie Maggie, secretly feel a let down, an anticlimax, knowing that you're less connected, involved and useful than before? Isn't there a void that you fear may be difficult to fill? And therefore, have you not an incentive to bolster your indispensability and retain a hold on Annie somehow?"

But the cynic's take would be awry. Auntie Maggie's sole motivation, as ever, was her surrogate daughter's well-being. Understandably, she couldn't be totally at ease while a risk remained that Annie's convictions could get out of hand.

On this and related matters did she deliberate as she drove back to Mumbles to collect the children from Dylan. She dwelt on her conversations with Annie over the last few days. Several times they'd revolved around Annie's contention that surely she'd been healed for a purpose. Of this, as of earlier twists and turns in Annie's revival, Auntie Maggie had been instinctively sceptical. But, unsure of how to react, she'd thought it best to soft-pedal, and had let Annie do most of the talking.

"I expect most people would say that I was healed so that I could preach his message. How would you describe his message, Auntie Maggie?"

"Well, I'd say that he preached modesty, humility and the Christian ideal, don't you think?"

Auntie Maggie had answered solemnly, all the while wondering why Annie couldn't simply cherish her recovery: why this determination to pursue St Cennydd's purpose?

"But preaching would be a problem for me, Auntie Maggie," Annie had persisted, "I wouldn't be comfortable sharing my experience with others or pressing my opinions on them, and surely St Cennydd would have known that. Don't you agree that he must have had something else in mind?"

Auntie Maggie had inwardly winced at Annie's familiarity with the saint, and yet, had been heartened again minutes later as Annie played with the children as naturally as could be.

During her drive, however, Auntie Maggie decided that she would try to put an end to her apparent complicity in unearthing St Cennydd's purpose. The time had come to challenge her niece's latest conviction; gently of course and always with her happiness in mind. She mentioned her intention to Dylan.

"I trust you, Auntie Maggie. You do what you think is best. You have my phone number in Edinburgh so give me a ring if you think I should come home early for any reason."

The tide was in and high when they parted.

"She's been well for long enough to allow me to take this chance," was Auntie Maggie's opinion as she drove home to Rhossili, "I'll help her and Peggy put the children to bed and then bring up the subject after Peggy's gone home."

"Where did you go on your walk today, Annie?" was Auntie Maggie's opening.

"I went to Llangennydd church: that's where I feel like going these days. Actually, I hadn't been home very long when you arrived with the children."

"Did you happen to see St Cennydd?"

Annie froze on her way to the fridge. Auntie Maggie had no idea how she'd react. As it was, she turned to her aunt with a classic smile, delightful dimple and bright brown eyes, her head and shoulders tilted forward in a gentle reprimand.

"You're teasing me, Auntie Maggie. Of course I didn't see him… but whenever I sit on that bench in the lych-gate a peaceful feeling comes over me."

This didn't surprise Auntie Maggie: she believed in the power of association, wherein a feeling experienced earlier is linked to a particular place and circumstance.

"Actually, I've grown to depend on those quiet moments," continued Annie, "They reassure me that St Cennydd's spirit is still my friend, and now and then I do need reassurance Auntie Maggie. You see, I don't expect another face-to-face encounter like the one I had at the spring."

So impressed was Auntie Maggie by Annie's candidness and reasoning that she deviated from script.

"What are these peaceful feelings like, Annie? How do they affect you?"

Annie was clearly pleased by her interest.

"It's so hard to explain, Auntie Maggie, but let me put it to you this way. I've felt a bit like that when I walked out of a cinema after watching a film which had warmed me, inspired me; I felt as if my cares had gone away and I couldn't think badly about anyone. You know what I mean, don't you?"

Auntie Maggie nodded and Annie continued.

"Well, those feelings never lasted long, but the ones at the lych-gate have a stronger effect which seems to last forever."

Auntie Maggie was enthralled, but she forced herself to pursue her plan.

"Do you think the spirit will be with you for the rest of your life, or will be there be a time when you get over this business, this business with St Cennydd, and just accept that you're well again?"

Annie's face reflected surprise and disappointment. It then relaxed, and Annie moved to hold her auntie's hands.

"Auntie Maggie, you've been so wonderful to me; I wouldn't have survived without you, so I'm sorry that you seem to be upset. But, you know, I can't help the things that have happened to me. The most important thing, as you say, is that I'm well again, but you don't believe it's a coincidence, do you?"

In the face of Annie's generosity, Auntie Maggie felt mean-spirited... in the face of her conviction, quite ordinary. She saw herself as a second-rate hack overshadowed in a drama by a brilliant star. At that moment her challenge seemed futile but, ignoring Annie's question, she continued with her agenda.

"But do you have to stick with this idea that you've been healed for a purpose?"

"Why else would I have been healed, Auntie Maggie? Was it just the luck of the draw? I can't believe that. And because one favour deserves another in return, I'll do anything that St Cennydd wants me to. You don't blame me for thinking like that, do you?"

With earnest brown eyes, Annie pleaded with her aunt to see things her way.

"I'm sorry, Annie! I do understand what you're saying, but I can't shake the feeling that you're taking this too far," and then quite innocently, as a throw-out line, "And because of our differences on this, I sometimes think you'd be better off without me now."

"Please don't say that, Auntie Maggie."

Auntie Maggie was taken aback by Annie's reaction: she was visibly upset. She begged again, this time with her head to one side and hands held in prayer. The ease with which it seemed Annie's self-assurance had been dented threw Auntie Maggie.

"Promise you won't say that again… please!" Annie pleaded, "Even though I'm convinced about some things, I can't see me going through with this without you. I need your support, Auntie Maggie."

The wave of maternal warmth that washed over Auntie Maggie reminded her vividly of the original summons to Annie's house and her niece's pathetic plea at that time.

"I promise, Annie, I promise," she said, again without truly considering the consequences.

Déjà vu, but what else could she do? Maternal warmth or not, she knew by now she'd lost the plot; frustration set in. Annie, however, appeared relieved and smiled shyly as if apologising to her aunt.

"I've got to tell you this though, Annie: I'm still worried that if you take this relationship with St Cennydd much further, the world, even your family, might have reason to think that you're cuckoo."

Annie was gradually regaining her animated self.

"Auntie Maggie, do you think I'm cuckoo? Look at me! I must admit that now and then I feel funny about what's happening to me, but I'm perfectly normal with you and with the children, aren't I? Even though I've had what you might call a spiritual experience… just like a born-again Christian, maybe… it's not like me to go over the top. Let me check on the children for a minute."

On her return Annie took Auntie Maggie's arm and led her outside to the garden. The Bristol Channel brooded in the grey, no Lundy on this languid day. As they strolled against a mauve mosaic of heather, Annie spoke of Dylan's imminent and welcome return, the prospects of rapprochement with her father, the pleasure she was deriving from doting on the children once again, and then, "I'm really sorry, Auntie Maggie, that I can't get over this need to return St Cennydd's favour. And there's another thing as well: perhaps in this case, one favour demands another," with a light emphasis on "demands".

"Can I ignore that possibility?" she continued, "And if I did and then let St Cennydd down, wouldn't you worry that he might give up on me? Where would I be then? On my way to another breakdown, more than likely!"

Annie had said all this as if in soliloquy, occasionally hunching her shoulders and often shaking her head; not once had she looked at her aunt, which was just as well because Auntie Maggie struggled to contain her emotions, the foremost of which was anger, directed at herself.

"How could I have missed that angle?" she berated herself, "I should have been aware that this tit-for-tat would occur to her eventually. Have I lost my touch?"

Suddenly, she longed for time to herself – to regroup and reposition. The ground had shifted too sharply for instant assimilation.

Her arm squeezed Annie's, and with far more composure than she felt, she said, "Come on now, Annie! St Cennydd was a Christian, without a bad bone in his body; no eye for an eye for him, I'm sure."

Annie squeezed back, as if content to leave the matter at that. Soon, Auntie Maggie left for home, mulling the situation. She had to admit that as always she'd been impressed by the warmth and conventional nature of Annie's general behaviour, but beyond that there was little but disappointment. Her challenge had flopped; no tempering of Annie's conviction and no dampening of Annie's enthusiasm for St Cennydd. To make matters worse, she, as a possible constraint on Annie had been compromised.

"After our chat today," she bemoaned, "I'll have to think twice before challenging anything she does or says. If I do challenge her, she might question her conviction, and perhaps in the process let St Cennydd down. And from what she said earlier, she'd be afraid that she'd have a price to pay, which to her would mean slipping back into depression. I'll have to be careful not to put her through that again… and I can't wash my hands of the whole affair because Annie says she can't go ahead without me; so if I distanced myself from her, I'd probably be pulling the rug from under her, with the same awful effects."

She sighed as she leant on the gate to her garden. Uncle Trevor approached.

"How's Annie?"

"She's great, actually! It's amazing."

And of course it was! On a burst of positive energy, she reminded herself that what really mattered was that Annie was still happy. Yes, it was amazing, and she'd been part of it – and still was; even today, she had reaffirmed her promise to support. Her misgivings would just have to coexist with her commitment to Annie's well-being.

# FIFTEEN

UNCLE TREVOR ALWAYS cooked the Sunday lunch; it was a ritual and a prominent patch in the quilt that was their marriage. This meal, Auntie Maggie had contrived to attend even during Annie's darkest days, and so she would this Sunday. She'd arranged to be at Annie's house at nine; Annie would go for her walk earlier today to accommodate her. As Auntie Maggie left home, the village and its environs were bathed in brilliant sunshine. After several weeks of changeable weather, the forecast now was for a drier, sunnier spell.

"When the weather's like this," thought Auntie Maggie, "nowhere beats this place... or this country, for that matter. The scenery's beautiful anyway but the sun certainly adds another dimension."

Annie's manner that morning perturbed Auntie Maggie.

"What's going on?" she thought, "Something's got into her."

Annie seemed nervous and defensive. As soon as Auntie Maggie had greeted the children, she was ushered out of earshot by Annie.

"What's the matter?"

Speaking quietly, and glancing towards the children, Annie responded, "Something strange happened last night, Auntie Maggie, but knowing how you feel about St Cennydd and me, it's hard for me to tell you about it, but I have to, Auntie Maggie," and here she checked the children again, "After what happened last night, I think I'm going to need you more than ever. Will you stick with me?"

"Oh, dear!" thought Auntie Maggie, "It looks as if I won't like what she's going to say."

While she braced herself for what could be a confrontation, she was reminded with dismay of the constraints she felt had been imposed upon her yesterday.

"Will I stick with her, though?"

Of course she would, with or without any influence.

"I promised you, Annie, didn't I? Now, don't worry. Just tell me what happened."

Despite this, Annie seemed hesitant.

"I dreamt about St Cennydd," she said.

"Oh, no!" thought Auntie Maggie, "But keep calm now," and then to Annie, "How did you know it was him?"

"Because he looked like the carving of St Cennydd on the gate of the church: quite old and bearded and, believe it or not, gulls flew around his head as he limped out of the lych-gate."

So far this was not so bad, but surely with Annie on edge and nervous there had to be something else.

"Are you absolutely sure that..."

"It was him, Auntie Maggie," interrupted Annie firmly, and then added ominously, "and there's another thing, I'm afraid."

She knew it! Auntie Maggie tensed as Annie whispered, "I know why St Cennydd healed me. I know what his purpose is."

"Well?"

With an apologetic expression, Annie said, "Please don't laugh at me, Auntie Maggie, but he wants me to have his baby."

As preposterous as was this notion, Auntie Maggie failed to dismiss it. She was reminded of her unease when the saint first appeared in the picture: it was as if she'd been tuned to expect the worst… and here it was! Still, logic just about prevailed: how could Annie possibly have St Cennydd's baby? Really! This was the question she began to ask when she was interrupted by Annie, who'd anticipated another.

"… because in my dream, St Cennydd picked up the baby from the basket in the carving on the gate and gave it to me, and the gulls did nothing to stop him. Then he introduced me to a young man who was with him… his disciple maybe."

Logic fared badly in the face of this symbolism, which couldn't be clearer to Auntie Maggie… or more disturbing. The more Annie developed her dream, the more anxious Auntie Maggie became.

"Have you seen this person before?" Auntie Maggie asked.

"No, never in my life, except…" and here she hesitated, "except in another dream several nights ago. It never occurred to me to tell you about it, but…" and Annie described a car, driven by a surfer, creeping by her as she'd struggled towards Llangennydd… presumably on the occasion of her spiritual experience.

Auntie Maggie had assumed that Annie had stumbled in a daze towards Llangennydd on that day. In that same daze, had this youth appeared, then? If so, he was a real person, and thus a real threat; grounds to fear for Annie, and all the more reason why she, Auntie Maggie, should puncture this poppycock now. Yet, caution counselled and caution prevailed, while her frustration mounted. She forced herself to ask the natural question, "What did he look like?"

Annie obviously sensed her aunt's discomfort; she spoke hesitantly.

"I suppose you'd say he was striking. He had short, very blond hair and his eyes were blue; his skin was nice, and perfect except for a mole on his left cheek."

"He would be irresistible" thought Auntie Maggie with disgust.

Her anger got the better of her.

"And I suppose he was lame as well?" with the emphasis on the "he".

To make matters worse, Annie took her seriously.

"No! Well, not as far as I know, anyway. I didn't see him walk in my dream."

Auntie Maggie was beside herself.

"Annie! Why in the world would St Cennydd want you to have his baby?"

"Well, you know it's not in my nature to be able to preach his message, but the baby, when it's grown up…"

Connie interrupted excitedly.

"Connor just beat me at snap, Mammy!"

Annie turned to her daughter pensively, picked her up, and applauded her selflessness.

That Annie too may be distressed by this latest dream did not occur to Auntie Maggie. She assumed that apprehension over her reaction to this preposterous twist was the cause of Annie's nervousness and awkward behaviour. Feeling drained, she said, "If you don't go for your walk soon, Annie, I'll be late for my lunch. Come to think of it, I'll take the children home with me for a change. Trevor will love that."

Connie cheered, while Annie peered at Auntie Maggie.

# SIXTEEN

CONTRARY TO AUNTIE Maggie's assumption, Annie had been horrified when she became aware of her dream, appalled at the thought of conceiving St Cennydd's baby, and repelled by the idea of making love to a stranger; she'd presumed the father would be a surrogate chosen by the saint. Later that morning while describing her dream to Auntie Maggie, she'd felt agitated and confused; a state of mind exacerbated by her aunt's increasing impatience and her own disappointment at the abrupt adjournment of their conversation. In consequence, she peered mournfully at Auntie Maggie as she kissed the children goodbye, and distress dogged her as she left on her walk.

"I still believe that St Cennydd healed me; what I can't believe is that he would ask me to do something like this. Why would he be so unfair… cruel even?" she bemoaned; one day, on a cloud, the next, weighed down by it.

In a while, however, exercise, fresh air, the warmth of the sun and the grandeur of Gower touched her to beneficial effect. The cloud lifted a little, allowing her to reason.

"If I find this idea so repulsive, I don't have to go through with it. And anyway, what about Dylan? I couldn't hurt him like that."

Yes, indeed! What about Dylan?

Prior to this dream, Annie had found her connection with St Cennydd not only supportive but also thrilling; her anointment had made her glow. Suddenly, though, she felt out of her depth.

"What have I got myself into? How could someone I trust

expect me to do something so awful? He must know I can't do it, so why ask? Is he trying to get rid of me, then?"

So, had St Cennydd not embedded himself in her psyche, becoming one of the pillars of her existence, Annie's revulsion at the saint's request would have led to a break with him by now. As it was, he couldn't be summarily rejected. Had he been, Annie, in effect, would be obliterating a part of herself, and not any old part but the one which she believed had delivered her from depression. And though she tended to agree with Auntie Maggie that St Cennydd would not trade in tit for tats, it would amount to the same thing should she deny him; for how then could she look him in the eye? How could she possibly expect to lean on him? And in the absence of his support, how far back down the slope might she slip?

"Could this be some sort of test to see if I deserve his protection? But that's unfair too because he knows I'm going to fail it. The thought of having this baby disgusts me, and anyway, I can't do this to Dylan... no, I can't do it."

An observer on Rhossili Downs would have found the vastness of the beach far below breathtaking. At that low tide, the beach would have seemed as deep as it was wide. Annie would have appeared as a helpless speck in an immense stretch of sand; this was how she felt as she approached the path to Llangennydd... much worse than she had felt when she'd left home. Knowing for certain now that she was unable to comply with the saint's request, she dwelt on the likely consequences; they weren't pretty. A recurrence of her depression was surely inevitable. That awful face would reappear and she and Dylan would remain apart; imagine the poor children's confusion. Her spirits sank and that familiar tension slipped into her stomach; the cloud that earlier had weighed on her bore down. Who could have imagined the emotional rollercoaster she would travel in the wake of Dylan's indiscretion?

"I should have known that this spiritual stuff was too good to be true. I'll just have to knuckle down again and fight, and deal with my demons the best I can… one day at a time."

She had done it before and would do it again if she had to; the prospect was daunting, though. She took the path which left the beach for Llangennydd.

"Why am I bothering to go to the church? I've turned St Cennydd down, so nothing will happen. I can imagine myself sitting on the bench, miserable and alone."

She continued to the church out of habit and proved herself wrong. Perhaps because her spirits were so low, the peaceful feeling that washed over her was, if anything, stronger than usual. The comfort she felt took her by surprise; she sat stock-still on the bench.

"So even though I've let St Cennydd down, his spirit is still my friend?"

She was touched by the spirit's magnanimity and inspired by its loyalty to her, but she also felt confused; she conversed with herself.

"How can St Cennydd be so unfair, though, asking me to do this awful thing?"

"More to the point, how can you say that he is unfair? He must know that you've turned him down, and yet he goes out of his way to raise you up like this."

"OK! Let's put it another way: how can a Christian ask me to commit adultery?"

"All I can say is that he must have his reasons and when someone is so good to you, shouldn't you make more of an effort to trust him?"

Annie had taken her first step towards complying with the saint's request. There was a short break before, "Why is St Cennydd still prepared to be my friend?" with the emphasis on "is".

"Maybe he's giving you another chance, or perhaps he wants to remind you of what you're about to give up."

"Hmmm. It could be that, I suppose. The way I feel now, why would I have even thought of cutting my connection with him? I don't suppose many are blessed in this way; I really should treasure this relationship."

A second step had been taken.

"But what about Dylan?"

To this she would resort repeatedly as she talked herself into agreeing to have St Cennydd's baby.

"When I think of how miserable I was on the way here, how can I not agree?"

A wave of sadness for Dylan washed over her. He'd be devastated, but what option did she have? She recalled her reception just now at the lych-gate and the remarkable lift she'd experienced. The risk in denying St Cennydd had become unacceptable; anyway, hadn't she told Auntie Maggie only yesterday that she'd do anything St Cennydd wanted her to? Yes, anything!

It was at this point that Annie almost took a leap of faith. She couldn't quite convince herself, however, that St Cennydd's compassion would guarantee protection for her and her family. Her feet couldn't quite leave the ground, exposing her to nervousness over what lay ahead.

"But surely St Cennydd is too generous to make me do something I might regret."

Again, slightly short on conviction! But wouldn't the saint's humanity ensure plain sailing during her unenviable task? Back and forth she went! She was regularly struck by the enormity of her role and the potential repercussions, and each time she sought encouragement from one of St Cennydd's saintly qualities.

It might be said that the saint's request really was a test of Annie's faith in him.

"If you do this for me," he seemed to suggest, "You will do so because you have faith in my judgment and confidence in my ability to manage the consequences for you."

Had Annie passed the test with flying colours, had she taken the leap, had she given herself completely to the spirit, conviction would have been her friend; she'd have feared nothing. As it was, she'd kept her feet on the ground, just about, and so, nervousness, uncertainty and sadness over Dylan weighed on her. And yet, whenever these feelings threatened to get out of hand, an appeal to the saint seemed to settle her. In this way, some calm was established in her mind, and although she couldn't quite believe in it, "trust in the saint" became her mantra.

Amidst these tug-of-wars at the lych-gate, Annie dwelt on Dylan's position. Since her healing at the spring, she'd wallowed in the warmth of being able to love him again. She'd looked forward so much to their reunion, but now a saint had put paid to that.

"Poor Dylan! He's suffered so much already and now he'll probably suffer more, despite what St Cennydd might do to smooth things over. I have to do my best to trust in the saint, that's all. To make matters worse, Dylan's expecting to come home soon; I've got to delay that. All this will be hard enough on me without having Dylan around."

It wouldn't be easy, but she'd phone him on his return from Edinburgh, and tell a lie.

"Dylan, I need more than a week on my own to adjust. Will you wait a little longer till I'm ready?"

This she could do only if the lie were white, which it certainly was, for what good would she be to him if perennially depressed?

"But he's bound to ask me how long I think it'll take."

This practical point emboldened her to address an aspect of her commitment to St Cennydd which hitherto she'd overlooked. The saint wouldn't expect her to suspend her life indefinitely, would he? Surely a fortnight would be sufficient for further directions to be forthcoming? And if none appeared in that timeframe, surely she'd be justified in getting on with her life, confident that she hadn't let him down, or betrayed him?

Surely this and surely that; obviously not entirely convinced! As she stood to leave for home the church caught her attention: impassive, yet impressive.

"I wonder if the feeling that wraps around me when I sit here would be stronger in the church?"

The possibility intrigued her but unnerved her also, and that's why perhaps she abruptly reminded herself that she ought to leave; Auntie Maggie was awaiting.

So, when she left the church she was off-balance and on edge, but knew that she'd agreed to have a baby; a baby that she presumed would be born to preach St Cennydd's message. But who would the father be? Who would serve as St Cennydd's surrogate? It would have to be someone special, one endowed with St Cennydd's qualities: his blond-haired disciple, perhaps? No, no! She couldn't be sure of that, so she'd await a sign, an irrefutable one; considering what was expected of her, there could be no room for doubt.

"Trust in the saint."

As Annie always did on leaving the lych-gate, she supped at the spring. Had she not been so preoccupied, she may have glanced at the pub. Many patrons sat outside, and among them were two she would have recognised… even from a distance.

Later, while picking up the children, she had no chance to confide in Auntie Maggie. It was a relief of sorts, because how would her aunt have reacted to her decision, she wondered? Tomorrow, though, she would tell Auntie Maggie everything: she had to… she needed to… her aunt's collaboration was vital.

It was early afternoon before Auntie Maggie could really focus on Annie's disturbing dream. After the children had left, she'd eaten less lunch than usual and rushed the washing up. Now, with time to herself, she felt as constrained as before, reluctant to act in the face of what seemed to be a mounting call to action. And yet, as frustrated as she was, she still managed overall to remain calm; she regularly reminded herself that even though she feared Annie would take her dream seriously, the threat from that blond boy was still unlikely to materialise, and that there was nothing wrong with dragging her feet until it became clear that she had no alternative but to act. Anyway, didn't she owe it to Annie not to abandon her supporting role sooner than was necessary?

"Should I phone Dylan? If I do, the first thing he'll ask me is whether he should come home. I don't think there's any need for that… not yet anyway. So why worry him."

Occasionally, the day's development did get the better of her.

"St Cennydd wants me to have his baby! Honestly! Can you believe it?"

How would Annie morally balance her mission with her

love and respect for Dylan? Whichever way, she would surely prefer not to have him around, and if so, how would this be reconciled with Dylan's expectation of an imminent reunion.

"She's got a whole lot of squaring to do," she thought.

But then, her counter routine would again kick in, and relative calm restored.

"It would be nice if I could confide in Trevor," Auntie Maggie thought, and in a way she did. Later that evening, and out of the blue, she volunteered, "If I seem to be quiet it's only because I've got Annie on my mind."

"But I thought you said she was doing well, and how amazing the whole thing was."

"Things never stand still with her, Trevor."

Trevor, well groomed and bespectacled, sat back in his chair and stared at her inquisitively, presumably wondering if at last she was giving him an opening.

"Why don't you get it off your chest, Maggie? Just tell me what's going on."

Auntie Maggie shook her head pathetically and whispered, "I can't Trevor, I just can't. What I can tell you, though, is that I wish I hadn't told her the story of St Cennydd."

Again, Trevor stared at her, intently this time. In return, she smiled wanly. Nothing more was said, but as Auntie Maggie reflected, Trevor regularly glanced her way, with almost certainly on his face a question, "What is St Cennydd's significance, pray?"

# SEVENTEEN

THE NEXT DAY, Trevor received a phone call from Arthur; a visit was out of the question as a result of the family feud. Even Trevor had spent much less time with Arthur recently; not only was he naturally upset by his brother-in-law's treatment of Maggie, but also appalled by his refusal to budge on Annie. Still, during the phone call he reluctantly accepted Arthur's invitation to have a pint that evening and, prodded in part by Maggie's minor revelations, he decided to use the occasion to once again appeal to Arthur to soften his stance on Annie. He'd give it one more go, and that would be it! Early that evening, they sat opposite each other at a table outside the pub. They'd already dissected the current cricket season. Now, they brooded over their beers. Trevor fussed with his tie, then nervously played with his pint, knowing his moment was nigh… while Arthur betrayed no emotion.

"You may think Annie's over the worst," began Trevor, nodding slightly while he spoke, "But I know for a fact that things aren't going that well."

Arthur raised his head, stiffened, and drilled his brother-in-law with a piercing gaze. Trevor sought solace in a drawn-out draught of ale.

"I can't understand why you won't talk to her," he continued, "It's bound to help the girl. It's time you grew up, you know. I must say I find your indifference…" and here he mixed metaphors, "… deafening!"

Arthur pounced on this incongruity and, whispering vehemently, immediately launched into Trevor.

"Deafening? What the hell d'you mean by that? Deafening? Anyway, why would I listen to you? You can't fool me, Trevor; you know nothing about Annie. Maggie hasn't told you a thing. Go on! Admit it! If I were you, I wouldn't stand for it. She might as well have castrated you."

Trevor was a good man, unassuming but comfortable with himself, his self-esteem bolstered by the close and loving relationship he'd enjoyed with his wife. Normally, his gentle nature would have handily absorbed this bombast from Arthur, as a willow would the wind, but he'd become less sure of himself since Maggie's contract of confidentiality with Annie. Although Trevor was now tolerant of her decision, he was still hurt by it.

"She might as well have castrated you," Arthur had said.

Trevor's appeal had been swatted aside and, to boot, his manhood questioned. He, more sensitive and less resilient than in the past, allowed pride into the picture. Having given Arthur the impression that Maggie had let him into the loop at last, wouldn't he lose face if he failed to confirm it? So, Trevor talked himself into divulging a minor revelation.

"Huh! She's told me a lot more than you think," followed by an embellishment laced with irony, "And only because she knows she can trust me. I'm sure she wouldn't mind me telling you, though, that Annie's problems revolve around that old saint called Cennydd."

So surreal was this assertion that Trevor fully expected Arthur to show surprise. Far from it!

"Well!" exclaimed Arthur, "What about that! It looks as if I'm on to something, docsn't it?"

Instead, 'twas Trevor who was taken aback; he fussed with his tie again and downed another draught before asking, "What d'you mean?"

"Well, I've been following her, haven't I? Not that it's been hard, mind you; she always ends up at Llangennydd church… that's St Cennydd's church, isn't it… just sitting in the lychgate. I've been watching her from the pub across the road for days now. So what you said makes sense; it means I'm on to something. If you won't tell me what it is, that's up to you, but I'll find out one way or another, you watch!"

What in the world was Arthur's motive for spilling the beans like that: a desire, perhaps, to rub Trevor's nose in the fact that he, Arthur, was as ever a step ahead? If so, it backfired badly, because Trevor's pride, at a stroke, was overwhelmed by disgust. To think a father would tail his daughter rather than nurture her as he ought to. Trevor, in what was for him a dramatic gesture, rested his chin in his hands, and staring at Arthur shook his head in utter disbelief. Then, he stood, buttoned his jacket, and left, to his companion's gloating giggle. Arthur's reaction suggested that he had no misgiving over anything he'd done or said. But why had he spilt the beans? Did he not consider them to be of consequence?

On his way home Trevor deeply regretted betraying Maggie's confidence. He felt so foolish at having let Arthur goad him to the point of telling. But he hadn't done that much harm, had he? After all, the so-and-so had already been aware of Annie's connection to St Cennydd's church. In his mind, not so much harm had been done as to not relate the incident, word for word, to Maggie. It was an uncomfortable experience, though she too shook her head in disbelief. When he'd finished, he was embraced by her.

"I am so sorry, Trevor. I know how hard this is on you. Even though I can't tell you more, I love you no less. Please believe me."

That she'd responded with such warmth and passion, when

he'd feared recrimination, was a wonderful tonic for Trevor. It had a profound effect on him: it cleansed him of his hurt.

When Trevor arrived home from his meeting with Arthur, Auntie Maggie, despite her calming routine, was still brooding over the day's developments. That morning she'd heard Annie's rationale for deciding to conceive St Cennydd's baby. The decision hadn't come as a surprise to Auntie Maggie, but to actually hear Annie elaborating on it had been chilling.

At least Annie had felt troubled by her decision and what it might entail. And, to tell the truth, Auntie Maggie was sympathetic to Annie's fear of relapsing into depression, but still, to proceed regardless of the consequences was foolish and irresponsible! If not for the fact that Annie, as usual, had been so affectionate and natural with the children – no, no, no! She should have challenged Annie anyway, even berated her, but had desisted, because she'd felt she needed time to craft a sensitive reaction. Auntie Maggie had left for home exasperated; at that moment, her dual roles with respect to Annie, of sustaining and containing, had seemed cruelly incompatible.

Naturally, she'd wondered whether to phone Dylan.

"I probably should, but then again, he'll be home in a few days... on Wednesday," and that's when it had struck her forcibly that should Annie need restraining, should her bubble need bursting, it would be much more appropriate and effective if Dylan did it.

"But she might get up to something in the next few days! I know, I know, but as long as I'm her confidante, Annie won't do anything without talking to me first; if she does bring something silly up, obviously I won't wait for Dylan then... I'll confront her myself."

As a result of these thoughts, Auntie Maggie had decided

that she could wait until Dylan's return to brief him, and because he now would be Annie's restrainer, Auntie Maggie had also decided that, barring a catastrophe, she could focus more on keeping Annie's spirits up: Auntie Maggie had experienced relief.

Still, at home that evening, awaiting Trevor's return from the pub, she had brooded… until galvanised by her husband's account of his drink with Arthur. She, too, saw her brother's behaviour with respect to his daughter as despicable, and in her disgust, became spontaneously and fiercely protective of Annie; Auntie Maggie once again was washed in a wave of maternal warmth. But should she tell Annie of her father's machinations? Knowing her brother, Auntie Maggie had little doubt that his leak had been deliberate. She refrained from saying so to Trevor: why needlessly cast him in the role of a pawn? But what advantage had Arthur in mind in disclosing? Here, Auntie Maggie racked her brain in vain. Still, she decided to tell: was it not better for Annie to be forewarned and, therefore, to some degree at least forearmed?

"I'll tell her tomorrow," and she did.

"But don't you think, Annie, you should stay away from the lych-gate? Go somewhere else where your father won't be able to spy on you."

"Auntie Maggie, you know quite well that the lych-gate is important to me now," spoken passionately by Annie, "Anyway, Daddy won't hurt me."

With this, Auntie Maggie agreed and, convinced by now that Annie would not be kept away from the lych-gate, she soon gave the visit her qualified blessing. At that moment, however, neither had grasped the likely consequence: not Annie, because her mind, already unsettled, was further agitated by this reminder of her father's tenacity and spite; nor Auntie Maggie, for she was suddenly taken by the satisfying thought of Arthur on the back foot.

"Whatever his reason for telling Trevor, he won't expect Annie to turn up as usual," she thought, "So when she does, he won't know what to think; it'll eat at him, for certain."

# EIGHTEEN

I T WAS LUNCHTIME on the same day, a Tuesday. Nursing his
half-pint and occasionally mopping his brow, Arthur sat
outside the pub in Llangennydd. Well, sat most of the time
anyway, for every now and then he'd pace awhile. He was
beside himself with frustration: for days he'd watched Annie,
just sitting in the lych-gate, all alone. She'd done nothing else; it
made no sense at all. It even occurred to him that she knew he
was there and was stringing him along. By yesterday he'd had
enough, so he'd decided to stir things up. Hence his invitation
to Trevor and his intention of revealing that he had Annie under
surveillance. He'd been rehearsing how best to spill the beans,
how to do so nonchalantly, but as it happened his brother-in-
law had paved the way. Arthur had hoped that his revelation
would have flushed Annie out, forced a change in her pattern
of behaviour, and perhaps precipitated a foolish move. But no!
Here she was again today, merely sitting in the lych-gate, all
alone. Surely Trevor would have told Maggie who then would
have passed it on. He conceded that perhaps Maggie had not
yet had the opportunity, but in his sour and surly frame of
mind, he chose to believe that Annie had been told and that
she was daring him to confront her.

"Dammit! This girl has been the bane of my life for weeks."

He hated not knowing what was happening: it ate at him.
All this time she'd kept him guessing, and here she was doing
it again.

"Well! If it's confrontation she wants, that's what she'll
get," but not yet, apparently, for at that point he took his half-
pint and strode inside the pub. The patronage was patchy, so

the innkeeper idled behind the bar. Preparatory to pumping him, Arthur paraded his charming side; how remarkable his chameleon capacity!

Then, "Have you noticed anything unusual taking place in the churchyard recently... or in the lych-gate?"

In the past, the innkeeper had been amiable but not overly chatty.

"I don't know what you mean, really, but anyway, from where I work here I can see the church but not much else. Why d'you ask?"

Arthur beckoned the other with a conspiratorial gesture, and in a whisper, concocted a sob story in the hope of disarming the innkeeper.

"Oh, it's to do with my daughter. I'm afraid she's in a bit of trouble. She visits this church quite often, but she won't talk to me about it. I'm worried sick about her, actually."

The innkeeper shook his head a few times but showed little emotion. Presumably, in his pub, behind his bar, like most in his line of business, he was inherently on guard with strangers who asked questions.

"Well, what about in here," continued Arthur in a whisper, "Have you noticed any changes, any new faces?"

"Don't think so," in a normal and polite tone, being obviously non-committal, but Arthur would not take heed; he persisted with his whispering.

"What about that chap over there, the one with the blond hair, dressed in a T-shirt and jeans? I've seen him here over the last few days. What about him?"

The innkeeper's face turned sharply towards Arthur; it expressed tension and suspicion. He replied frostily.

"Just a surfer. They often drop by."

As they spoke, the person in question, aware perhaps of

their scrutiny, glanced at them cagily, but on catching their eyes immediately reverted to reading a paper.

"Is he a regular? Has he been coming here for long?"

Shrugging his shoulders, the innkeeper was abrupt, "For maybe a week, maybe less."

With his eyes suddenly on fire and with an edge to his voice now raised, Arthur reacted, "But I thought you said you hadn't noticed any…"

"Hey! Hold your horses!"

The innkeeper had interrupted; how strange that he seemed to have doubled in size.

"Whose bar is this?" he said, speaking politely again now, "And, anyway, who's the one asking for favours?"

Arthur was wired to a short fuse. With his glass near empty, he stormed away from the innkeeper, shaking his head in disgust and dismissing him with a wave of a hand.

"Would you like another drink, sir?"

Strutting towards the window, Arthur ignored the question; why the dickens should he play the innkeeper's game and, anyway, his mind was now on another. As he passed the head of blond hair, no eyes were raised to meet his; the surfer kept on reading.

From where Arthur settled, facing the window, he could just make Annie out. He exhaled noticeably, shaking his head in exasperation. Little had pleased him today: no breaks in Annie's case, although he did wonder if this lad could be a lead. After all, his visits to the pub did seem to coincide with Annie's to the lych-gate. Now and then he glanced back at the surfer who remained glued to the paper. What caught Arthur's eye was not only the hair but also an unusually fine complexion. At his next glance the surfer was gone, but the paper remained on the table next to an unfinished beer.

"Gone to the loo, I suppose," thought Arthur.

He turned to check on Annie and wondered, "What on earth can be keeping her there?"

Suddenly, he was struck by a funny feeling. As he leapt to his feet he scraped his own chair noisily, and bundled others aside as he careered towards the back of the pub. Bypassing the loo door, he barged through another which opened onto a car park. At its far end, a car screeched as it made a hasty exit: it was black and beaten up, but its driver was obscured.

"Oh damn! I just knew it!"

Regardless, he returned to the window within the pub with a lighter step. That Annie had left in his absence fazed him not a whit. After all, something was happening at last. It seemed he'd unearthed a clue, and as a result his confidence grew, to the point that he approached the innkeeper, knowing that he was on a hiding to nothing.

"What can you tell me about blondie?"

The reply was as polite as it was predictable.

"Would you like another drink, sir?"

"Don't you 'sir' me," was Arthur's response. He slammed his glass on the counter and left in a huff, effectively banning himself from the pub for good.

Later, Connie, tiptoeing at the kitchen window, turned excitedly towards Auntie Maggie and exclaimed, "Mammy's coming."

"Thank goodness for that," thought Auntie Maggie, "I hope that nothing unpleasant happened."

As Annie crossed the road for home, however, her demeanour was not encouraging.

"She seems upset," thought Auntie Maggie; an impression confirmed later when she was motioned by Annie to a corner of the kitchen.

"It looks as if your father confronted you, Annie?"

"No!"

"What's the matter, then?"

Annie folded her arms around her aunt's neck, rested her chin on her shoulder, and whispered, "I didn't get that peaceful feeling today."

For the second time in four days, Auntie Maggie felt deeply disappointed, alarmed even, by her own naivety.

"Of course she wouldn't!" was Auntie Maggie's self-reprimand, "How could she, with her mind focused on Arthur?"

Auntie Maggie was on the verge of making this point when Annie continued.

"I had realised, actually, as I walked above the beach that I might not get the feeling with Daddy so much on my mind. I even kept on telling myself that it was asking too much to expect it to happen every time. Despite that, though," and here Auntie Maggie felt Annie's head shaking deliberately, "when it didn't happen, I was surprised by the effect it had on me. It really upset me. And of course everything was made much worse knowing that Daddy, prowling up there at the pub, was behind it all."

For a moment, Auntie Maggie saw Annie's setback as an opening to make a rational case. Her instinct was to build on Annie's doubts; absent those feelings at the lych-gate, Annie would question her connection with the spirit. Without a spirit, no relationship with the saint and, of course, no baby... but she recoiled at the thought of where that might lead. In line with her decision yesterday, she soon embraced her supporting role. Annie was hugged affectionately, and as if that was all she'd sought, she disengaged from it with a smile, albeit wan.

"Thanks, Auntie Maggie! I can't tell you how important

you are to me. You see, I thought I had this… what you might call… unusual situation under some kind of control, but after this afternoon I'm not so sure."

Again, Auntie Maggie fleetingly considered a challenge, but how could she take the risk? And, anyway, she'd delegated that role to Dylan. Annie's face pleaded for Auntie Maggie's support, which was gained; no room for containment here!

"I know I should be stronger, but I am worried that I won't get that peaceful feeling again. That doesn't say much for my faith in St Cennydd, does it… and to be honest that worries me too."

Annie smiled pathetically at her aunt.

"Do you think I'll get that feeling tomorrow?"

What option had Auntie Maggie for now but to solidly support her niece?

"Of course you will."

She did admit to herself, however, that Annie might not should she still be focused on her father. In her mind, Auntie Maggie thrashed around for something to support her claim, but failed. Her discomfiture was quelled by Annie.

"I think I'll go inside the church tomorrow. I've wondered before if those peaceful waves I feel would be stronger in there."

Auntie Maggie leapt at this lifeline.

"That's a great idea, Annie, and you should go there earlier. Get there before your father arrives. That way he won't be on your mind. You'll be fine, you'll see."

"I think you may be right, Auntie Maggie."

"Of course, I am! You know quite well that you didn't stand a chance today, but it'll be different in the church tomorrow."

Gradually, colour returned to Annie's pretty face, and the children were comforted with a long and warm embrace. As

Auntie Maggie readied to leave, Annie said out of the blue, "D'you think Dylan will be upset if I ask him for more time to myself?"

In response, Auntie Maggie's emotions were all over the place, but she managed a firm reply.

"No, of course he won't! You know Dylan."

"Yes... I know him. He is special and he couldn't have been more understanding. I've said before that if ever there was a saint, it's Dylan."

Yesterday, Auntie Maggie had left Annie's house exasperated; today she was calmer, her sustaining role clearly in the ascendant.

"Don't forget, Annie! I'll be here at eleven tomorrow."

# NINETEEN

As if the bay and beach which sweep between Rhossili and Llangennydd aren't striking enough, they are complemented by a green and unspoilt raised strip of land which runs parallel to them. It in turn nestles into Rhossili Downs which towers above. The strip resembles a massive bench and conjures images of sitting giants bathing their calloused feet in the sea and resting their backs on the downs. The strip is bare but for one small cluster of structures in which a white house stands out. This is the old rectory and is positioned roughly halfway between Rhossili and Llangennydd because the same clergyman used to serve both parishes. Not far away lay the original village and church of Rhossili. During the thirteenth century, devastating sandstorms hammered those coastal parts of Gower which face south and west. Rhossili's inhabitants, threatened by dunes, were forced to re-establish their community and church where they stand today; safe from the sand but still walloped by winds. It is said that the present church's south doorway, with its famous chevrons and side shafts, may have been the chancel arch of the original Norman church in the dunes.

Neither of these, however, was the church that occupied Annie's mind as she paused near the old rectory on the day following Auntie Maggie's pep talk. Llangennydd was the one on her mind, but especially her fear that when she reached it she'd be disappointed. She hadn't slept as well as usual. She'd lain awake for about an hour in the dead of night: demons had sprung to life. They'd wormed their way around her brain sowing seeds of doubt; they'd punctured her reservoir of optimism. Annie had fought back the best she could, but rarely does the dead of night present a level playing field. By morning, Auntie Maggie's confidence building had largely been undone, and Annie had found herself resorting regularly to "trust in the saint".

"If I don't get that feeling today, not even in the church, where do I stand then?"

In Annie's mind, this visit to the church was evolving into a make-or-break situation.

"And if I do get the feeling, will it be as soon as I walk through the door, or should I expect to sit down for a while?"

While she paused by the old rectory, she took several deep breaths, as she would many times before arriving at Llangennydd's village green. There, she was sufficiently aware to scan the surroundings several times before being assured that her father had not yet arrived. Then, she hurried to the lych-gate. Was it any wonder that no special feeling washed her there, given her preoccupation with her father; to Annie, however, fearing the worst, it was another indication that she may be on a fool's errand. For a moment, she even considered going no further, but as it had earlier, the church impressed her; so solid and obviously sacred, a sanctuary, without doubt.

Yet, it was with heart in mouth that she followed a path down a gradual incline past weathered gravestones to the half-open doors of the porch. Within, it was shadowy, but light enough to reveal a metal ring which she assumed would unlatch the church door. In her nervous state, Annie was affected by everything: put out by the tightness of the ring, taken aback by the weight of the door, surprised by the light let into the nave by south-facing windows, and much disconcerted to find someone seated in the church, on the right, halfway to the chancel. Should she leave, she wondered; nothing would happen in someone else's presence.

"Perhaps I should come back tomorrow. Why put myself through this?"

And yet, she did, for it had dawned on her that, despite everything, there was something in the air within the church which gave her a modicum of peace – just as her visits to Burry Holm had offered a slight release. Annie sat on a pew on the aisle, behind and in line with the other person. Whoever it was had narrow shoulders, sat erect, faced straight ahead, and wore a blue T-shirt and a tight-fitting form of skullcap.

"Funny not to take it off in church," she thought, followed by a plaintive "Shouldn't I be going? What's the point of me staying here?"

The point was that she sensed that once she was outside, the small comfort she felt would likely evaporate. After twenty minutes of this balancing act, the person up front arose. Not wishing to appear rude, Annie bowed her head as if in prayer, and may have remained in that pose had it not become plain that the person approaching did so with a limp. Curious now, she squinted upwards as unobtrusively as possible – to be shocked!

"Good God!" she thought, "It's that young man who was with St Cennydd in my dream."

Annie gasped involuntarily and raised her head to fully face the person; a shy glance was all she received in return. The rhythm of a limp persisted until the church door behind her to the left clanged closed. Still in shock and breathing quickly, Annie pictured a young man with striking blond hair, blue eyes and a fine light brown complexion marred only by a mole on the left cheek. And then she whispered, "It was him, St Cennydd's companion... it was him, and he's lame as well."

Annie slumped in her pew; she was awestruck. She'd just been handed a sign which couldn't have been clearer. As far as she was concerned, the events and visitations of the last week had coalesced and climaxed in spectacular style. She now knew exactly what was expected of her. A baby, which she would carry, would be fathered by this blond, blue-eyed young man – St Cennydd's surrogate – who was lame just like his mentor; she was expected to make love to him – and she would – soon. Over the past few days, faced with such imminence, Annie may have unravelled, but this irrefutable and powerful sign had wrought a remarkable change in her. Its mysticism had so impressed her that she'd become convinced of St Cennydd's compassion, and was certain that it would insulate her from harm; she was absolutely sure now that in return for her compliance, he would ease her way and protect her family. So, at last, Annie took a leap of faith; she surrendered to the supernatural. No longer would she feel sadness for Dylan, nor would she need Auntie Maggie's support. In fact, with respect to the sign she'd been handed today, her aunt would be kept in the dark: why complicate things by telling her? She, Annie, would simply do what she had to. She would give herself to this young man whose appearance struck her now as reflecting saintly qualities; she would give herself in the certainty that all would be well. Her feet had finally left the ground, and she felt no fear. It occurred to her that her disappointment at the lych-gate yesterday had probably been part of a plan, one that had encouraged her into the church today to be delivered to her destiny.

While drinking at the spring she determined to revisit the church tomorrow, confident that the young man would be there again; a tryst would then be arranged. As she was about to leave the green, and despite her exalted frame of mind, it occurred to her to scan the surroundings for her father.

"I can't see him anywhere. I wonder what happened to him today," she thought, but she didn't dwell on it. She left for home walking on air.

At that moment, as Annie left the village green, Arthur was motoring back towards Llangennydd, climbing the final rise in the road which would then tumble into the village; he was livid. Half an hour earlier he'd followed the exact same route and had pulled into the pub's car park. Though effectively banned from the inn, he'd had no compunction parking at the back of it.

"No sign of that surfer's beaten-up, black car," he'd thought, "I wonder if I've scared him off."

He'd arrived at the village earlier than usual to select an alternative spot where best to spy on his daughter. The chosen station was in the shadow of a wall at the east end of the church, where every minute or so, indifferent to the scrutiny of curious passers-by, he'd peeped over the wall towards the lych-gate and then around it towards the road along which Annie would arrive. Suddenly, he'd straightened.

"Good God! There's the surfer after all. He must have come from the church, I suppose. And look how lame he is!"

Arthur had then made two mistakes: he'd shouted "Hoi", alerting the surfer who reacted by scooting towards the pub and darting through the door with surprising mobility for one with a limp; compounding his error, Arthur had followed inside, barrelling across the bar, only to be blocked imperiously by the landlord at the exit that led to the car park.

"I've had enough of you," as softly spoken as he'd been the day before, "Now, get out of here the same way you came in and never set foot inside again; d'you understand?"

What could Arthur have done? Without a word he'd wheeled and, dismissing the landlord with a wave of a hand, bustled back to the door from whence he'd come. As he'd arrived at the wing of the pub, totally out of breath, he just spotted the getaway car's tail disappearing around a bend just up the road.

"Damn! He must have had another car today, and now I won't know which one."

Arthur wondered why he felt so winded. Despite this, he'd given chase in his car; all in vain though, and now he was returning angrily to the village, just after Annie had left for home. Not even Arthur had the gall to use the pub's car park again. Instead, he followed the road down an incline past the church and parked some way down there. He returned to his previous station and resumed his spying routine. After just over half an hour, with still no sign of Annie, he left for home, frustrated.

"Well, at least it looks as if I've made her change her routine," he fumed, but even on this observation he'd soon be proven wrong. Out of curiosity, Arthur drove past his house in Rhossili and snaked down through the village. On the way back he was shocked to see Annie approaching on the path from Llangennydd.

"She was there after all? Why didn't I spot her? I suppose she might have been in the church as well. Good God! Don't tell me she's hanging around with that surfer?"

Arthur decided to confront his daughter.

"I'll tell her what I know – that should shake her up!"

He parked opposite Annie's home, exactly where the path met the road, and stepped outside with a flourish; his body language spoke of aggression. Annie, however, approached apparently unperturbed, her bearing full of confidence. She took no notice of her father, and was about to skirt his car when he stepped in her way with a swagger.

"You've got a nerve! You think you can act like this and get away with it?"

His voice was threatening, but Annie, seemingly unfazed, moved to circumvent him. Arthur reacted by grabbing her dark green top.

"After all I've done for you, you'd think I'd be treated with some respect," he spat at her, "Anyway, what the hell are you doing hanging around with that surfer?"

Annie, her face by now betraying concern, struggled to free herself, prompting Arthur to tighten his grip… until a thought occurred which caused him to glance towards Annie's house; that's when he let her loose, albeit roughly. Annie jogged away, waving tentatively towards her kitchen window which framed Auntie Maggie's very worried face. Arthur cursed his sister. He slumped into his seat and drove the short distance home, humiliated but more determined than ever to unearth exactly what was going on.

Annie was greeted enthusiastically by her children; not so by Auntie Maggie.

"Are you all right, Annie?" with concern, "Did he hurt you?"

Shaking her head, Annie replied in a matter-of-fact manner, "No, not a bit. I suppose he was frustrated that he'd missed me at the church, that's all."

Annie's calmness and apparent pragmatism surprised Auntie Maggie. In her judgement, the scene that she'd just witnessed had been extremely confrontational. How could Annie not be shaken? Auntie Maggie pointedly eyed her niece before continuing the conversation.

"What about that peaceful feeling, Annie? Did it happen in the church?"

Annie smiled warmly and nodded.

"Yes! You were right all along, Auntie Maggie," she said, and yet, absent was the enthusiasm that Auntie Maggie would have expected, given Annie's apprehension when she'd left for the church that morning.

"I would imagine," Auntie Maggie thought, "that relief would show all over her face, but it doesn't, does it? What's going on, I wonder?"

Again she gazed at Annie, this time with suspicion. An edge to her voice reflected her unease.

"Now that you feel confident about the spirit again, you'll still have to wait for a sign, I suppose?"

"Yes," was all that was said to that, but then, "Auntie Maggie? Would you mind if I left you to play with the children?"

At a stroke, Auntie Maggie's concern ballooned into acute anxiety. Clearly, Annie was withholding and, worse, seemed not to care that her aunt was well aware of it. Suddenly, not only did Auntie Maggie fear for her niece but for her own reputation as well. Up until now, despite mounting evidence that Annie may be losing her grip on reality, she'd refrained from intervening forcefully for fear of destabilising her niece's mental health.

"The worst might not materialise," Auntie Maggie had often reminded herself, "So until it does, aren't I justified in dragging my feet?"

But, if now, as it appeared, she was out of the loop, gone for good was the option of deferring confrontation; suddenly, she couldn't afford to wait for Dylan's return.

"Given her obsession with this baby," Auntie Maggie thought in a mild panic, "she may be on the verge of ruining her life, and of course I'd be to blame as well."

Auntie Maggie did not doubt that she'd taken her role as Annie's confidante seriously, but had her judgement been awry? Should she have already poured cold water over Annie's convictions regardless of her frame of mind? A cold sweat brushed her at the thought of her culpability should Annie do herself irreparable harm; who else could be at blame when for the last few days she alone had been put in the picture? Admittedly, to have been chosen above all others by Annie had been a privilege, but such status rarely comes without consequence, which in her case, at this time, was dread that she could be partly responsible for destroying Annie's life.

By such dire ruminations Auntie Maggie was moved to act resolutely.

"Connie! Mammy and I are going outside for a minute, all right? You'll be able to see us through the window, don't worry. Come on, Annie!"

Don't worry? How could Connie not worry as she would notice Auntie Maggie's gestures becoming increasingly emphatic?

"Annie? You're hiding something from me, aren't you?"

No reply.

"I should be encouraged, I suppose," thought Auntie Maggie, "that she can't lie to me," and then to Annie, "How can I advise you and protect you if you won't tell me everything?"

No reaction from Annie; she stood perfectly still, gazing at her aunt as if nothing of significance had been said. Auntie Maggie raised her arms and shook her head in frustration. Her one consolation was that in view of her niece's composure, she'd no reason today to tread lightly.

"Look, Annie! If you follow through with this baby, you're going to ruin your life... all of our lives. Surely, you see that?

Dylan will be devastated, and you'll be the laughing stock of the village... and of Gower for that matter."

Auntie Maggie took a deep breath, placed her hands on Annie's shoulders, made eye contact at close quarters, and appealed with every muscle of her body.

"Annie, I do understand your fear of relapsing into depression, but if you have sex with some stranger... and I suppose it'll be that irresistible blond-haired boy you dreamt about... the mental pain you'll suffer will be far worse than what you went through when you were depressed."

Auntie Maggie couldn't justify that statement, but she'd said it anyway, and it was followed by what she'd dared not say before.

"And for you to think you're doing this for a saint who's been dead for over 1,400 years! You're out of your mind, Annie; you're making a fool of yourself. Do you realise what harm this will do to the children? I don't know!" in exasperation, and then in a slightly more conciliatory tone, "Now, I agree that your experience at the spring may have been special, but it was nothing that can't be explained. We've gone over this before, I know," but Auntie Maggie ran through it again, regardless. Annie held her aunt's gaze but expressed no emotion. In light of her recent hypersensitivity, Annie's indifference to this onslaught confused and alarmed Auntie Maggie. What more could she do? What more could she say, other than make a personal appeal.

"You've no idea how much you're hurting me, Annie, by cutting me off like this. The last few weeks haven't..."

She was interrupted by an obviously sincere and lingering embrace from Annie, who whispered, "Auntie Maggie, you needn't worry. Everything will be fine."

So extreme was Auntie Maggie's reaction that even Annie,

at last, seemed perturbed. Wrenching herself out of her niece's embrace, Auntie Maggie exploded, her typically warm and gentle face on fire.

"That's exactly what worries me, Annie. Somehow you've convinced yourself that everything will be fine regardless of what antics you'll get up to. I'm frightened, if you really want to know!"

Then, in a quieter voice, with head bowed and shaking, she continued, "I've lost you, Annie, and I can't deal with the responsibility on my own any more."

Abruptly, she straightened, waved limply at Connie in the window, and left.

"I hope you'll still take care of the children tomorrow, Auntie Maggie."

No reply from Auntie Maggie as she headed home to tell it all to Trevor – tell him every detail, tell him every nuance – and then phone Dylan in Edinburgh.

# TWENTY

TREVOR WAS RELIEVED that Maggie had at last confided in
him. No longer would ill-feeling lurk; once again their love
would be whole and uncomplicated. For that he was thankful.
At the same time he was aghast at Annie's plight and surprised
that Maggie would have allowed the situation to deteriorate so.
Her balancing act may have been commendable just after the
experience at the spring but, surely, restraining Annie had been
called for before this? Normally, their close relationship would
have demanded that he reveal at least a hint of his disapproval,
but how unkind would that be with Maggie obviously upset?
Rather, he, well groomed, bespectacled and nattily dressed, held
her hands with the earnestness of a newly-wed and reminded
her of how adeptly she'd steered her niece through the most
difficult of periods.

"You've been brilliant," he reiterated, "You only gave her a
long leash because you were in the know, but now suddenly
things are different, aren't they?"

It was clear to Trevor that Maggie had been shaken by Annie's
eerily assured demeanour, and clear too that she, in confiding,
was not only sharing her load but also seeking advice and
direction. Though not a natural leader, Trevor took control.

"Obviously, she's got to be stopped, Maggie. We've got
to protect her from herself, and as you suggested, it's just as
obvious that Dylan's the one to do the job, so let's give him a
ring at his hotel."

Maggie agreed that it would be better if she found the
fortitude to tell Dylan what had happened since he'd left, and it
was she now who rang him.

"I doubt that he'll be there, though. Dylan O'Kinnon, please!"

She was told that Dylan had checked-out that morning.

"We should have realised that," was her frustrated reaction.

Next they phoned Dylan's office in Swansea and left a message for him with the receptionist urging him to phone them as soon as he could. They left a similar message at Dylan's hotel in Mumbles.

"Let's go for a short walk, Maggie. It'll do us good – it'll clear our heads."

As they strolled along the old rectory path, sea breezes tempered the afternoon heat while Trevor reasoned with Maggie, seeking to ease her mind.

"Annie won't do anything today. She'll stick to her routine, you'll see, and leave for Llangennydd church tomorrow as usual."

"She won't be able to go, Trevor, if I won't look after the children."

Trevor stopped and as he thought he stared out at the sea.

"If you don't look after them, Maggie, she's bound to give them to somebody else. Anyway, don't you think it's a good thing for us to stay in touch with her and keep an eye on her? I know you're upset with her but I think you should make the effort."

Maggie nodded and Trevor returned to his reassuring role.

"Of course, Annie could have already arranged to meet someone on her walk tomorrow, and head for Burry Holm, for example. I think that's very unlikely but, just in case, I'll watch to see which path she takes. If it's to the beach, I'd be worried, but if it's the old rectory, then she'll probably be aiming for the church. In any case, I'll drive and park wherever I have to, so that whichever route she takes, I'll be able to watch her."

To their irritation, Dylan had left a message in their absence. He couldn't leave Edinburgh as early as he'd thought. This meant an overnight stay in Crewe, so he wouldn't arrive in Swansea until half past ten tomorrow morning. Because he hadn't heard from Auntie Maggie, he assumed that all was well with Annie.

Maggie in particular seemed upset over the change in Dylan's plan, or was it the sting in the tail of the message that had got to her?

"What do we do now, Trevor?"

He adjusted his glasses and straightened his tie as he rethought the situation.

"Let's think this through together, Maggie. Dylan should be back at his office by quarter to eleven tomorrow morning, and he's bound to phone us straightaway. Assuming Annie heads for Llangennydd church and is meeting someone there, Dylan needs to get there before her, that's all. If she leaves here at eleven, she'll get there about twelve, right? That should be easy for Dylan. If his train is late or for some other reason we don't hear from him in time, I'll go to the church myself and take care of the situation… if needs be. Now, if it's obvious she's going to the beach, then I'll confront her there, on my own or with Dylan if I have the time to meet him at the church beforehand."

Unheroic had been used by many to describe Trevor Williams in the past, but was he ever a hero now! Maggie, on tiptoe, embraced him. What a relief it must have been to have her husband in the mix at last! They then took what practical steps they could to – in Trevor's words – protect Annie from herself. From their front window her house was visible, so why not keep vigil together, Trevor suggested.

"I know Annie won't leave now but why not keep an eye on her anyway?"

He suggested as well that Maggie phone Annie later, after Peggy had paid her daily visit.

Trevor was nervous that evening. He took heart, however, from one fact: Maggie's balancing act was dismissed for good; restraint was now the key word. Regardless of what might follow, Annie obviously had to be stopped in her mission to have that baby, and by tomorrow he was reasonably confident she would be; therefore, he was hopeful, but apprehensive all the same. For the first time in weeks he sat next to Maggie on the same settee after dinner; he did his best to concentrate on his book. Now and then he touched her hand; his heart took a leap as each time she touched him back. He couldn't believe how lovely it felt to be really nice to her again.

Meanwhile, Annie was living on a much higher plane, as if her leap of faith had been taken from the crest of Rhossili Downs, where then she was caught by a magic carpet which now swept her effortlessly through the day and life's minutia. She felt elevated by her now undoubted spiritual connection, and fortified as well.

So there she was cocooned, insulated from reality, imbued with certainty, and devoid of fear: a recipe for disaster, Auntie Maggie would have said. For Annie, however, this "dangerous cocktail" afforded her an ideal state of mind. How fabulous it felt being sure of oneself, so special and serene… and as a result, incapable of being anything but generous to others. Connie and Connor were the main beneficiaries, but so too was her mother when she paid her daily visit. Annie sensed with pleasure her euphoria rubbing off on her mother, as if her own state of mind was infectious. Later, to her surprise, Auntie Maggie phoned. Annie was overcome by the love she felt and keenly aware of how indebted she was to her aunt. She decided not to be the first to mention St Cennydd and, as Auntie Maggie desisted, their conversation was confined to small talk, mainly about the children; how nice it was once again though not to be openly at odds with her.

"Will I see you at eleven tomorrow, Auntie Maggie?"

"I'll be there, Annie."

That night Annie went to bed on her own, yet acutely aware that she wasn't alone.

# TWENTY-ONE

D URING BREAKFAST THE following morning, Auntie
Maggie poked at her porridge and played with her eggs
on toast: she was understandably still on edge, despite pledge
upon pledge from a patient Trevor that their plan was virtually
watertight. "But what if" refused to yield. Even the prospect of
their plan's success failed to fully please, for how could she be
at ease should Annie relapse into depression?

Three phone calls shaped their morning. During the first,
around nine, they were informed that Dylan had indeed
contacted his office, but earlier that morning when no one
was around. His phone message had confirmed that he should
arrive in Swansea at half past ten. Trevor nodded with a thumbs
up at Auntie Maggie and then impressed on the caller that
Dylan should phone them in Rhossili as soon as he arrived at
the office.

"So far, so good," as he smiled at his wife and relayed the
information, "He should make it to the church in time."

Auntie Maggie felt encouraged: after all, something at last
had gone right. Buoyed by this news, she suggested that they
spend the next ninety minutes tidying the front garden. Annie
could not but notice them, and their presence might trigger
a call to her conscience. As they bent, then stretched and
straightened, they were hailed by a neighbour now and then,
but not a whiff of Annie. Regardless, they stuck to their task:
mowing, hoeing, dead-heading; feeding, weeding, watering
– till the phone rang!

"But it's only half past ten," gasped Auntie Maggie as she
struggled to her feet, "It looks as if his train was early."

Both hurried inside, leaving implements strewn around the garden.

"Hello?" breathlessly.

"It's Annie, Auntie Maggie."

Completely taken aback, Auntie Maggie was lost for words.

"Auntie Maggie? Are you there?" asked Annie, "Oh, good! Just to make sure that I don't run into Daddy at the church, I'm leaving now. Connie will be fine on her own for a few minutes, but please come over as soon as you can."

"Annie, please don't go yet," Auntie Maggie begged, "I want to talk to you," and the line then went dead. Auntie Maggie, still emotionally taut, was thrown by this unexpected twist in events. She scurried towards the front door, furiously beckoning Trevor to join her. She fumbled a few times with the latch, but it wouldn't have made a difference: Annie was already crossing the road in her customary green top.

"Annie! Come here!" at the top of her voice.

Her niece's response was a confident wave as if nothing was out of order; she then disappeared down the path.

"She's bound to be there before Dylan now. What shall we do, Trevor?"

She immediately felt foolish in the face of Trevor's calmness. In her defence, the balancing act she'd conducted, if only for a week, would have strained stronger nerves than hers. Trevor, however, was fresh to the fray; he laid his hands on her shoulders.

"Maggie, go to the children quickly, and I'll drop down the path to see whether Annie took to the beach or aimed higher."

In a few minutes, Trevor confirmed the latter.

"That's good news, Maggie. As for Dylan, he should still be able to make it to the church in time… just don't talk to him for long when he phones, that's all. And if for some reason he doesn't phone, I'll do my best to take care of things."

As before, the thought of Trevor in reserve comforted Auntie Maggie, although deep down she knew that Dylan's intervention would be much more effective; a surprise appearance from him would surely shake Annie free from her convictions.

"I better go now and get out of these working clothes," from Trevor in conclusion, "Dylan will phone soon, you'll see," and at twenty to eleven he did. Auntie Maggie, after asking the children to amuse themselves, took Dylan's call in the hallway.

"Hello, Auntie Maggie. Uncle Trevor thought it would be better if I spoke to you. It's about Annie, isn't it? Is there something wrong?"

"There may be, Dylan. Listen to me carefully now."

There was no time to waste so she told him bluntly of Annie's recent pressing need to reciprocate St Cennydd's favour by agreeing to have his baby.

"If you can believe that, Dylan! What she says is that she's afraid that if she snubbed the saint she'd end up depressed again."

"But why didn't you phone me, Auntie Maggie?" in an angry tone, "I told you I'd come home early if anything went wrong."

"Dylan, please calm down. I would have phoned you," with an emphasis on "would", "but I thought I had things under control… until yesterday when Annie's manner changed completely. It frightened me, to tell you the truth. I have to assume that she's about to meet somebody and do something silly."

Dylan interrupted again, this time with understandable curiosity. Auntie Maggie wasn't in the best frame of mind herself but somehow found the strength to insist on sticking to her bare-bones story; she'd fill in the picture later, she said.

"She must be stopped, Dylan… as soon as possible, and we think you're the one who should do it: you'd have the greatest impact. I hate telling you this, but there may be a young man who'll serve as St Cennydd incarnate, if you know what I mean," and here she shrugged her shoulders and shook her head. She then described the young man as striking, with short but very blond hair, blue eyes, and a perfect complexion but for a mole on his left cheek. This was followed by silence, which perturbed Auntie Maggie.

"Surely he hasn't hung up," she thought, and then, "Dylan?"

"Auntie Maggie," he replied, in a tired tone, "This is a hell of a shock for me; I want you to explain things a bit better."

She would have much preferred to reach out to him and comply with his request. After all, Trevor was ready in reserve, but this was no time for sentiment, and in her view, better by far that Dylan be the one to intercede.

"Dylan," she spoke in a firm voice, "There's no time for explanation. Can't you see how serious this is? And I was depending on you! Now, I admit I can't be sure that they've arranged to meet, but by now we can't take any chances, Dylan. If they do meet, it'll probably be in Llangennydd church… or Burry Holm, perhaps. Anyway, it does look as if she's going to the church today, so you've got to be there by half past eleven… and confront her."

In light of Auntie Maggie's vagueness, Dylan would have been justified in continuing to demand some answers, but he didn't; presumably, in acceptance of the situation's urgency, he saw no choice but to stumble into the relative unknown.

"All right, Auntie Maggie, I'll leave straight away. It's lucky that my car is at the office."

Auntie Maggie felt for him. She could imagine his confusion, disappointment and anxiety, so all the more her admiration when he added, "I'm sorry for snapping at you. That wasn't very nice especially after everything you've done for Annie… and for me."

Well! She wished she'd been able to do more, for as things stood, a satisfactory resolution was unlikely.

As it happened, Gower Road was chock-a-block with traffic. By the time he arrived at Sketty Cross, Dylan knew that he wouldn't be in Llangennydd by half past eleven; naturally, this added to the turmoil in his mind. Although the vagueness of parts of Auntie Maggie's report could have offered Dylan hope, the initial shock had left him open to a pessimistic interpretation of her tale. In the mix of his emotions were confusion – over Annie's behaviour – disappointment – over his decision to travel to Edinburgh – and anxiety.

"I had a feeling that another domino would fall. Jesus! Am I still paying the price for my slip-up?

For a while, Dylan sought solace in self-pity, and who could blame him? For several days he'd looked forward to a reunion with Annie, a prospect made all the more attractive when contrasted with the uncertainties of the previous month; weeks of unease, then days of delight and now this! Riven by an emotional rollercoaster, why wouldn't he pity himself, particularly in view of the sordid characteristics of this episode? And yet, by the time he got to Killay, one of the certainties in his life – that bedrock of trust which underlay his relationship with Annie – jostled for recognition, broke through the miasma of self and set him thinking along relatively more generous and optimistic lines.

Throughout Annie's troubles, not once had Dylan blamed her for his attendant tribulations, not once had his anger been directed at her. His tolerance stemmed from a conviction that Annie would not deliberately harm him, and even more germane to the current crisis, that she could no more be unfaithful to him than he could be to her. He still insisted that his indiscretion had been thrust upon him, and should the story he'd heard about Annie be anywhere close to the mark, then hers would have been thrust upon her as well.

And so he reasoned, until a wave of doubt washed over him again.

"Am I being naive?" and in this way did his mind see-saw; each downer, however, was eventually deflected by his instinct to give Annie the benefit of any doubt. There just had to be a satisfactory explanation for her highly unusual behaviour. Indeed, Auntie Maggie had touched on one, but to him, uninformed, it had thrown up even more questions.

An apologist for Dylan might pipe up here and point out that had Dylan not seen himself as the victim in the Marlborough affair – had he, on the contrary, lusted or set out to let his Annie down – it would have been virtually impossible, especially under the circumstances, for him now to completely trust her: those with dishonest traits are likely to assume the same in others. The guilt that Dylan had experienced after he'd admitted the affair to Annie stemmed not so much from the incident itself but from its aftermath; and that guilt would surely have resurfaced during his drive had he not been consumed by events and the danger that Annie was said to be in.

He still wished that he'd persisted with Auntie Maggie

though. By now, it troubled him that he knew so little of what had gone on. Questions multiplied in his mind: what was he to expect in Llangennydd? How would Annie react to him? What would it take to restrain her? Was this blond boy for real or not? Had he arranged a meeting with Annie already? Would he, Dylan, be forced to fight this fellow, and in that event, how would he fare? So many imponderables, but one thing however was clear: he'd be at least ten minutes late arriving in Llangennydd.

# TWENTY-TWO

ANNIE STRODE WITH purpose, parallel to and above the beach; a sky with clouds on the fly and an ocean alight with streaks of white formed the backdrop. To this, though, she was indifferent; the only cloud to have caught her attention had been poor Auntie Maggie's distress when she, Annie, had left home earlier than expected. But it, too, had floated by in the face of her conviction that her aunt would eventually see things her way.

Earlier that morning, Annie had awakened to a calm feeling; she'd known she would. Still in a cocoon and removed from reality, she'd brewed, imbibed and performed her ablutions. Intense was the warmth she'd felt for the children; she was particularly touched by the obvious pride with which Connie had agreed to take care of Connor – if only for a few minutes. Now, on her way to the church, she was imbued with certainty, still devoid of fear, she felt special and serene, her course was crystal clear. Without doubt, St Cennydd's surrogate, a blond, blue-eyed young man, would await her, and the spirit would lead her to him. A tryst would be arranged, and the die would be cast; she would soon reciprocate St Cennydd's favour and he would see to it that she felt at ease while she made love to a stranger, and he'd take care of the consequences as well.

How could Annie – a normally sensitive, loving and loyal lady – have undertaken such an outrageous mission? How could she have contemplated even touching this blond-haired, blue-eyed stranger? Her uncharacteristic behaviour had to be attributable to her recent mind-wrenching, massive emotional swings. Just think! First, it was bliss, then hurt; next, obsession, and the abyss of depression for weeks, followed by the joy of being healed. More recently, a plunge into uncertainty again; she'd had to struggle with an unenviable dilemma: whether to comply with St Cennydd's preposterous request or risk near-certain relapse; an illusory dilemma to others perhaps, but painfully real to her. Now imagine her huge relief having taken a leap of faith – her discomfort dismantled, her life in the hands of a saint who'd chosen her above all others. After all she'd been through, why would she question her state of serenity? Why wouldn't she continue to yield to the spirit? What reason was there not to complete her commitment to St Cennydd? As a result, Annie, without qualm, was acquiescing to adultery as she skirted the old rectory… on her own, yet acutely aware that she wasn't alone.

Snooping wasn't Trevor's cup of tea. He found its inherent unfairness unappealing; all his life, he'd ceded underhandedness to others. He couldn't fathom how Arthur could snoop on his daughter. And yet, despite his disdain for the practice, here he was, a little way down the caravan park, snooping on his niece.

"But only for her own good," was his genuine justification.

In keeping with his inexperience, he'd made no effort to fit the part; he'd made no concession to the occasion so as to better fade into the seaside scene. Amongst the caravaners and campers, Trevor stood out like a beacon, dressed in a light blue blazer, shirt and tie, and formal shoes. As he waited for Annie, he averted his gaze from those sufficiently brazen to stare at him. He feigned a nonchalant air by admiring Rhossili Downs and polishing his extra-thick spectacles with a handkerchief which he never failed to have at hand.

"There she goes! Good Lord, she's walking fast. At this rate," glancing at his watch, "Dylan won't get there in time. I better not let her out of my sight, then."

Trevor's discomfort in this unfamiliar role was ratcheted up a notch. He felt nowhere near as confident as he had while comforting Maggie.

"How close should I stay to her? Having to follow her is bad enough, but imagine how I'd feel if she caught me at it!"

Trevor needn't have worried: the road from the caravan park to Llangennydd consists of reasonably long stretches, allowing him in his car to keep Annie in sight at a safe distance. In the village, the road takes a sharp-angled turn to the right and then heads directly for the church. As soon as Annie rounded this bend, Trevor sped to it and parked his car on another road which angled uphill to the left. Trevor had never been thought of as a physical specimen, but he was slim and lithe for his age. Surprisingly quickly, he hurried back to a point in the road from where Annie could be seen entering the lych-gate and then disappearing down a dip to the porch.

"I can't see Dylan anywhere, but I'd be surprised if he'd made it anyway. So I better follow her, I suppose."

The prospect perturbed him. Snooping was anathema to Trevor, and so was confrontation.

"Shall I challenge her in the church, or wait for her outside?" was the question. He'd rather not enter, but would he then be breaking his vow to Maggie? Would she consider his pledge fulfilled if he hung back at the lych-gate?

"Good God! There's Arthur! He must have seen Annie going into the church. What will he do now?"

Trevor scurried across the road, where an arc in a few houses concealed him from Arthur. Carefully, he nosed ahead till his brother-in-law just became visible.

"Look at him! Like a wild dog on a leash! It's obvious he can't decide what to do. What should I do? I don't think I should interfere while he's there."

Delivered from his dilemma by Arthur, Trevor relaxed a bit.

For a brief period in the porch, Annie's poise was challenged. For some reason the stiffness of the latch ring on the door reminded her of her weakened state the day before. Once inside the church, however, her resolve was restored, for in the very same spot as yesterday sat a person, the same person… the same pose, clothes and skullcap; she'd known that he'd be there. Annie shivered at the thought of the spiritual climax which his surprise appearance had triggered yesterday. For a moment, Annie sat on a pew and reflected on how perfect it was that St Cennydd should be represented by such a beautiful boy, and with limp to boot. Suddenly, she felt the atmosphere in the nave to be so powerful and pervasive that she swore that she could stroke it. She was in awe of the moment and felt honoured.

Judging her dark green top to be inappropriate for the occasion, Annie removed it quietly, placed it on the back of the pew, and smoothed her short, long-sleeved white blouse. A practical question arose as she edged up the aisle.

"Will he be the first to talk? Will he greet me? He's got to be expecting me, although I must admit he wasn't sociable yesterday."

She settled on the end of the pew directly across from the surfer, whose head faced forward; a shy glance was the only acknowledgement Annie received. It looked as if she would have to instigate, after all.

"Hello," she whispered.

The response was another shy glance and a mouthing of "hello".

Still riding high and emotionally on fire, Annie's expectations of this meeting were intense: innocuous exchanges failed to fit the bill. She took a more intimate tack.

"Why do you come here so often?"

"Because this is St Cennydd's church and I look up to him for inspiration," spoken still facing forward.

Thrilled by this reference to the saint, Annie thought, "I can't believe it. Everything is falling into place," until she was struck by something, something so preposterous as to be impossible.

"Say that again, please," in an urgent tone, and the surfer did, facing Annie this time.

"You're a girl!" with Annie's voice raised in alarm, "You are a girl, aren't you?" with the emphasis on "are".

"I don't know exactly what you mean," in apparent confusion.

"Well, I… I thought you were a man, but it's obvious from your voice that you're not. You are a girl, aren't you?"

"Yes! Of course I'm a girl, but what's so bad about that?"

A trapdoor might as well have opened under Annie. The wind was sucked out of her, her magic carpet came crashing down to earth. So stunned was she that not a thought was given to the confusion regarding this person's sex.

"I can see now," Annie might have reasoned, "how this girl could have been taken to be a boy. Despite her fine complexion, her hairstyle is a boy's and she's no breasts to speak of; she's always dressed in trousers and a T-shirt, and of course, people naturally associate surfing with men."

With this in mind, we recall Annie stumbling to Llangennydd in a trance-like state, and we can understand how the surfer would have registered in her subconscious as a young man, and then would naturally have appeared as a young man as well when presented as St Cennydd's disciple in Annie's subsequent dream. Even Arthur had taken the surfer to be a boy despite several sightings. The publican who served Arthur, however, had known better for the surfer had often ordered a beer. This explains the publican's frosty demeanour after Arthur had referred to the surfer as "him".

No such thoughts for Annie, however, for in her state of shock, hers were fixed on "She's a girl" and the revelation's obvious implications. Annie's hands came up to cover her face, her train of thought predictable.

"This is awful! It's obvious I must have made the whole thing up! But I was so sure of my spiritual experience! Well, this girl makes a mockery of that – and my so-called commitment to St Cennydd. I've only got myself to blame; I should have listened to Auntie Maggie. She told me I was out of my mind hanging my hat on a saint who'd been dead for fourteen hundred years. How stupid I've been! So there's no saint taking care of me, after all."

This was as far as she got before bursting into tears; Annie's shoulders shuddered. Thoughts were impossible; if only the same could be said for feelings, for none of hers were pleasant. She eventually rose to hurry back down the aisle without a glance at the surfer. Totally deflated, Annie felt foolish, commonplace and vulnerable once again. How suddenly things can change, especially for the worse; to think that not much earlier, she'd glowed and had felt serene and special.

Annie's breakdown had appeared to galvanise the surfer: she'd been shaken it seemed from her shyness and then transfixed by the hysteria across the aisle. At one point, she'd moved to touch Annie, but retracted. As she watched Annie lurching towards the exit, her expression was one of hurt, as well as concern. The door clanged resoundingly, and then a soothing silence shrouded the church again. It was now the surfer's turn to bury her head in her hands. Soon, she too cried, but quietly.

With Arthur in his sights, Trevor had relaxed a bit; he occasionally straightened his tie. He hoped that he was doing the right thing not following Annie into the church.

"Arthur can be so difficult, but you've got to hand it to him: if he's not tenacious, he's... now what's going on?"

Annie was seen to return in a rush to the lych-gate. Arthur stood and appeared to try and block her, only to be pushed aside like a punch bag. He recovered quickly, but too late; Annie had opened the gate and was hurrying back in Trevor's direction. This was his cue to retreat, and he did so with alacrity, despite his years... and formal shoes. Eventually, he turned uphill towards his car and hid in a back lane. Soon, Annie could be heard approaching, spluttering and talking to herself.

"What could have happened," Trevor wondered, "Something must have gone terribly wrong, but surely if Annie's upset, isn't that good news for us? No, no! I can't be sure of that, but I wish I could let Maggie know what's going on."

Further speculations were cut short as Annie jogged into view.

"Good Lord! Where's her green top? Don't tell me she's been attacked!"

Arthur followed on Annie's heels, clearly labouring, while gesticulating and berating his daughter.

"What's wrong with him, I wonder? I would have thought that he'd catch her easily."

Around the bend the pair disappeared, with Annie still

spluttering and Arthur ranting and gasping for air. Trevor resisted the immediate urge to tail; he reasoned that Arthur, in particular, might do a U-turn. It struck him with amusement that he was beginning to think like a snoop. When he eventually followed them around the bend, he chose to do so on the outside curve. He stopped suddenly and recoiled; he'd seen Arthur, leaning forward with his hands on his knees, on the side of the road, a mere ten yards away.

"What shall I do now?"

He had wondered if he should force himself to visit the church. The idea had made him uncomfortable, so it was with mild relief that he decided that he had no choice but to follow Annie, now that she'd dropped Arthur. In hand with this decision, however, came another reason to fret.

"I can't drive by Arthur. I'll have to offer to pick him up. That'll be no picnic! He'll browbeat me to death."

Trevor needn't have worried: Arthur was strangely subdued. He wasn't his tyrannous self, at all.

# TWENTY-THREE

D YLAN'S YELLOW RENTAL car stood out at the east end of the church. He'd parked it untidily, not far from the spot where, twenty-four hours earlier, Arthur had peeped over and around the wall in vain. Ten minutes late, as predicted, Dylan had legged it through the lych-gate, past weathered, neglected gravestones to the porch. He'd driven the length of Gower largely oblivious to the views. He had managed to hold onto his belief in Annie, but the stream of imponderables had continued to weigh on him; he was at a loss of how to assess so much of what had happened. As the church's heavy door creaked open, he had little idea of what to expect and even less of what he would do. Dylan was physically strong though; if this came down to a scrap, he thought he'd be able to hold his own. Annie's dark green top draped on the back of a pew caught his eye and compounded his unease.

"What on earth could that mean?" as likely scenarios buzzed through his mind. Several more were spawned when he spotted the surfer, slumped and all alone.

"Could that be the chap who Auntie Maggie referred to? He looks small from here; he's hardly the threat I thought he might be, but there, I don't know what's going on. What a relief though that Annie's not with him. Oh, but she may be hiding somewhere, I suppose!"

Dylan picked up the top and trod up the aisle, choosing to sit on the same pew as Annie had. The surfer glanced at him briefly.

"Good God! He's crying. I can't believe he's so slight, but I must admit he is good looking. And there's the mole on his left cheek. 'St Cennydd incarnate' Auntie Maggie had said; I don't know about that, but he definitely is the one."

Confronted with a mere weeping waif, Dylan's confidence rose; his mind settled down and focused on what was now his main concern: Annie's whereabouts.

"D'you recognise this top?"

For a moment he feared unresponsiveness, but then came a glance and a nod.

"Do you know the lady who wore it?"

This time, just nods.

"Was she here earlier?"

Again a nod midst gentle sobs.

"D'you know where she went?"

A shake of the head was all he got. Dylan, frustrated now and keen to engage the other, asked the obvious.

"Why are you crying?"

This worked, for the surfer, still sobbing gently, straightened, and facing Dylan said pitifully, "There's no point me telling you: I know you won't understand."

Then, forward slumped the surfer again, head now on an arm on the back of the pew in front. Dylan had done a double take; he was flabbergasted but energised as well.

"You're a girl! You are, aren't you?"

Dylan stared at her, shaking his head in disbelief. He was only a little less in the dark than earlier and none the wiser about Annie's whereabouts, but now he knew the surfer was a girl, he experienced huge relief; he felt almost happy, certainly happy enough to be able to focus on the surfer's concerns, even in the face of his own. Her obvious anguish reminded him of Annie's during their last few weeks together.

"Where is Annie, I wonder? I really should leave and try to find her, but shouldn't I try and coax some information from this girl… and anyway, I can't leave her like this; she's a mess… for some reason."

Dylan was endowed with empathy, a natural consoler was he. That he'd failed to help Annie get over her problems attests to the insidious and devilish nature of her adversary at that time. Now, in the nave of St Cennydd's church, he knelt by the sobbing surfer and would have taken her hand had he not at the last minute deemed it overfamiliar.

"Please don't be upset. Things are bound to get better soon."

There was silence but for the surfer's sobbing. Her head continued to convulse gently, until she gradually settled down.

"Will you help me find that lady?" and then pleading with more passion, "Please help me!"

Softly spoken and facing Dylan, she replied, "Why do you want to find her? What does she mean to you, anyway?"

That the voice was a girl's still threw him; his former mindset held some sway.

"She's my wife."

The surfer sighed; her head returned to rest on her arm. Eventually, she sat up and said in the same soft voice, "It's time you left to find her. I'm sure she's walking home and more than likely on the trail above the beach. What's her name, by the way?"

Dylan was taken by surprise: he thought she would have known Annie's name.

"It's Annie. What's yours?"

"Sarah."

Sarah stood and entered the aisle; Dylan was shocked to see that she limped.

"How long have you been…?" as he glanced awkwardly at her feet.

"All my life."

What a strange experience this had been! Now, a reply so simple but packed with pathos moved Dylan to the point that he sought a gesture to express his sympathy. This time he thought it not inappropriate to hold her hand, and he did so until they came to the church door. Beyond, the shadowy porch, weathered gravestones and lych-gate failed to register with Dylan: his eyes were on the girl. There appeared to be something on her mind: her focused gaze and furrowed brow betrayed as much. She seemed more alert as if she'd shed a layer of sadness.

Just as Dylan was thinking, "I need to find Annie now, so should I say goodbye?" the girl stopped, looked up at him, and asked, "Do you know this place well?"

Dylan shook his head, "Not really."

"You better follow me then. I'll get my car from behind the pub and drive to where I'm almost certain she's gone."

Dylan was impressed. As upset as she seemed to be, he would have thought that she'd prefer to be alone. Once in the seat of his rental car, he took several deep breaths, and shook his head in amazement. As he followed the girl around the bend where Trevor had spied, and along the road where in Annie's mind a gaggle of gulls had been her guide, Dylan reflected on the last fifteen minutes; that the surfer was a girl had been a huge relief. Gradually, however, a wider perspective reasserted itself. It was true that the crisis surrounding Annie seemed to have been defused for now; Auntie Maggie probably need worry no longer. And yet, with relief came reality and a recognition that Annie, more than likely, was troubled again; and who was to blame for that? Dylan winced internally and did so again when reminded that Annie's strange behaviour remained unexplained. Had she really been hell-bent on making love to a stranger? Here, Dylan groped for that bedrock of trust which underlay their relationship; at times, like now, it was harder to grasp than at others.

"And will Annie want me back now or does this murky business muddy the waters all over again? Oh, Jesus! Think of the stuff we've been through. Look out! She's braking."

Sarah had stopped just shy of the entrance to the caravan park. Stepping out of her car, she beckoned Dylan to join her.

"There's the path she probably took. If you go along it you're bound to see her in the distance. See that little space there by the office?" and she motioned towards the caravans, "You can leave your car there if you're not going to be long."

And that was exactly where Trevor had parked after picking up Arthur earlier. To put his mind at rest, Trevor had then followed Annie on foot, formal shoes and all. Arthur, feeling out of sorts, had been left in Trevor's car, where he'd rested – until the surfer now drifted into his line of vision. Needless to tell, all hell broke loose. Arthur's car door swung open wildly. As he struggled to get out, he leant against the horn inadvertently, alerting Sarah who was on the move before Arthur got into his stride.

"I'm going to lock myself in my car. Please don't let him near me."

Dylan in the dark! Was Arthur involved in this as well? No mention had been made of him in Auntie Maggie's version of events. As Dylan braced himself to restrain Arthur, Sarah's door slammed shut.

"Arthur, what are you…?"

He stopped mid-question. Arthur had collapsed at his feet to a shrill scream.

"Good God! What's happening? This is awful," and as he knelt to comfort Arthur, he motioned Sarah to join him. She, ashen-faced and obviously shocked, complied.

"Go to the office and phone 999, and if there's anyone there with first-aid experience, ask them to come here as fast as they can."

Dylan failed to find a pulse. He cursed his refusal over the years to acquaint himself with even rudimentary emergency procedures. Nevertheless, amateurishly and frantically, he pumped on the open hand which he'd laid on Arthur's chest; still no pulse, as far as he could tell. He resumed pumping, while begging Arthur to respond. To his relief, a young man dashed out of the caravan park and with Dylan's acquiescence took over.

"There's an ambulance down there in the car park," was Sarah's breathless contribution, and just as she arrived back at the scene, a siren was heard in the near distance. A further rush of relief for Dylan, but this reflected more the transfer of responsibility away from him than hope for Arthur's recovery; truly, even Dylan could tell that things looked pretty bleak.

"Poor Arthur!"

He was suddenly struck by sadness.

Meanwhile, the young man methodically did all he could to resuscitate Arthur. He was heard to express pessimism as the ambulance screeched to a halt. Three paramedics emerged at the double and, following a brief assessment, one of them said, "We need to take him to Morriston Hospital; we'll work on him as we go."

"I'll meet you there," was Dylan's immediate response, "I'll follow in my car in a minute."

Sarah showed surprise at this, until diverted by Dylan who suggested, "It may be a good idea for us to get our cars out of the way."

She nodded and grimaced repeatedly towards Arthur as he was stretchered away.

"This is terrible," she muttered, "I feel I'm to blame for this."

"No, that's silly. How can you say that?"

"Well, it's obvious. Who was he chasing when he collapsed?"

Nothing that Dylan said could dissuade her from this view. It was clear she was reassuming the layer of sadness she'd earlier shed. And yet, she did manage to seem grateful when Dylan thrust forward to open the door of her car. Following a three-point turn, she nosed away from the scene. Dylan waved, she waved back, but she wept as she swept down the hill.

"God, I feel sorry for her, but what has she got to do with Arthur? And what was he doing here, anyway?"

One of the medics enquired of Dylan's relationship to Arthur. After they'd told him gravely that they held little hope for the patient, Dylan phoned Peggy with the news, commiserated earnestly but briefly, and urged her to meet him at Morriston Hospital.

"Call a taxi, Peggy, and hurry!"

Auntie Maggie was next: she was shaken, and there followed expressions of shock.

"Annie's probably walking home along the old rectory path," said Dylan, "Look out for her, would you Auntie Maggie? It would be nice if the three of you went to meet her."

"Did you see Trevor?"

"No."

Dylan hung up, nonplussed. So Trevor was involved as well? He then slipped into his yellow car, as blue as could be.

Sarah's story: children can be so cruel. At Sarah's primary school, she'd been mercilessly teased for being lame; so deep was her hurt that later, when boys made no bones about her beauty, she'd reacted defensively. As a result, with time, she'd been spoken of as frigid, and then, those same boys, their own defensive mechanisms flaring, had also made fun of her limp – and her underdeveloped breasts.

Her reaction had been threefold. She'd cut her hair very short in an attempt to avoid attention. Next, she'd taken to visiting the church at Llangennydd in the hope that its founding father, himself so famously lame, would provide inspiration; surfing, though a challenge to one with a limp, had followed naturally from her visits to the village. Finally, she'd questioned her sexuality, not out of any conviction but in reflection of her unfortunate history with men. Such was Sarah as she'd turned eighteen, having just left her secondary school to train as a baker with her father.

A week later she first saw Annie walking along the beach. Sarah was energised; her infatuation was immediate, adding fuel to the fire of her sexual ambiguity. Annie's figure was never fully discernable but it pleased Sarah all the same; even less of her face was on view, but Sarah was certain it was lovely. That Annie was shrouded in sadness was vital to Sarah's feelings: it encouraged her, as did, in those early days, the one-way nature of the relationship. Key to sustaining her crush was the daily visit from the lady in green.

For the next few weeks, the rhythm of Sarah's life had been set. A passion unrequited is more often than not corrosive; not so in Sarah's case. For the first time ever, she'd felt love for another. That she was capable of such emotion was exciting and, importantly, the parameters of the relationship were within her comfort zone.

This, till one day, Annie had seemed to be in difficulties: she'd slumped on the sand and then shuffled away from the beach. Naturally, this had troubled Sarah, but emboldened her as well. She would use Annie's plight as a crutch to take the plunge; she would introduce herself to the object of her affection. Disappointingly, she'd been treated with indifference, but at least at last she knew for certain that Annie's face, despite distress, was lovely. An emotional rollercoaster had ensued, culminating in Annie's shocking breakdown in the church, Dylan's subsequent generosity and Arthur's collapse. She bore no resentment towards Annie: for her first love, Sarah would forever have a soft spot. Interestingly, Dylan's timely gentleness had touched her; but for her father perhaps, no other man had treated her with such respect. These experiences had begun to bring her out of herself; she was gradually gaining confidence.

# TWENTY-FOUR

LATER THAT EVENING at Annie's house, all of the family gathered; Auntie Maggie had already tucked the children up in bed. Sadly, but as expected, Arthur had died. Auntie Maggie, Trevor, Dylan and even Peggy were by now fully up to date on Annie's experiences and her disappointment earlier in the day. The four would have gained from grieving as a group and also individually, as each came to terms with their feelings for Arthur and their recent dealings with him. Instead, they were forced to focus on Annie. She was obviously very upset; it seemed the issues that bothered her were threefold: first, her responsibility for her father's demise; how could she possibly live with that? Second, her shabby treatment of Dylan; how could he ever trust her again? And finally, the collapse of her connection with St Cennydd: without him to lean on, she'd already relapsed into depression.

Peggy moved to comfort her; kneeling by Annie's chair, she held her bowed head.

"Don't be so hard on yourself, darling."

Annie's head reared, her eyes radiating anger.

"You don't have a clue, Mammy," spoken bitterly, "You've no idea what I'm going through," immediately followed by regret, apologies in profusion and a theatrical hug for her mother.

"I'm sorry, Mammy. I hope you can understand why I'm so touchy. Anyway, I think I better go to bed and let the four of you talk about Daddy."

Trevor shook his head to a long, long sigh, adjusted his glasses, and straightened his tie. Dylan flopped back in his chair, mindlessly massaging his hairline.

"How pathetic she looks," thought Dylan, "I don't suppose she thinks anymore about those fifteen stupid minutes in Marlborough, but I'm afraid that doesn't let me off the hook, does it?"

As wearing as was Dylan's guilt, as badly as he felt, there was a sliver of a silver lining: he'd expected anger from Annie for intervening in her affairs without invitation, but all she'd expressed was remorse over her intention to be unfaithful. Shortly after Annie had left, Auntie Maggie spoke.

"Remember Dylan that we decided to give Annie a fortnight to get better and if she didn't, we would take her to her doctor?"

Dylan nodded. A few weeks earlier Auntie Maggie had been reluctant to seek professional help but that she was the one to bring this up now suggested a change of attitude.

"And you know that fortnight is up?"

"Yes… I do, Auntie Maggie."

After a pause, Peggy said, "Go and see her, Dylan. Try to cheer her up."

"OK! I don't suppose I'll do much good, but I'll give it a go."

"You're being unfair to yourself, Annie, assuming responsibility for your father. I think… and everybody else does too… that your reaction to him was perfectly fair. I agree with you one hundred per cent. If it was stress that killed him, then he brought it upon himself."

Annie sat up on her bed, looking downcast.

"Well, I didn't help matters, did I?"

"Annie, I just told you that he brought it upon himself. And, as for hurting me, you can't take the blame for that because I'm partly responsible for everything that's happened."

One may have thought that Dylan's guilt would have been allayed by Annie's adulterous intentions, but as he saw it, he was partly responsible for them as well.

"Mind you, I still think that what happened in Marlborough was definitely pushed on me, and d'you know what? I'm certain... absolutely certain... that whatever you might have done would have been pushed on you as well. That's the only rational explanation, Annie, because if I'm sure of anything, it's that you and I would never deliberately hurt one another. So don't be concerned about the two of us, all right?"

Annie smiled wanly and shook her head.

"Oh, Dylan! You are so nice, but I'm afraid that not even you can help me. My situation's hopeless. You see, St Cennydd is the real problem. Sit down, will you Dylan? This will sound ridiculous to you, and please don't be hurt by it, but I know I can't be well without his support. In my mind it was the saint who got me back on my feet. After that, I never felt alone, but now that I know I dreamt the whole thing up, where does it leave me, Dylan? It leaves me where I was before, and that was no fun, believe me."

Clearly frustrated, she tapped her fists on her forehead and then banged them on the counterpane. Dylan couldn't imagine how she felt.

"And there's another thing: now that St Cennydd's out of the picture, how long will it be before I'll have to deal with the face again. Remember the face? In any case, because of it, I can't let myself feel warm about you, Dylan. I just can't take the chance."

Annie slumped but then straightened again, as if reminded of something.

"Still, I would like you to stay in the house tonight. I probably won't feel strong enough tomorrow to talk to the children about losing their grandfather, so I'd like you to do it."

This was a pleasant surprise.

"If that's what you want, Annie, I will stay."

"But please don't think you can get close to me," Annie had continued, and then shaking her head, "I am so, so sorry about this."

Suddenly Dylan felt fatigued.

"I think I'll go to the kitchen now, Annie. I'll come back and see you soon."

No comment to that from Annie, but she did, however, have something to say. On her face, an appeal, an earnest appeal, had replaced what was earlier pathetic.

"It's important to me, Dylan, that you don't think I'm off my head, so I need to tell you this. Even though it's clear after what happened today that I dreamt this whole thing up, at the time I was certain that I was blessed by a spirit at the spring. I was, honestly! I needed to tell you that because I don't want you, of all people, to think of me as cuckoo."

Despite the joy he'd felt just under a week ago on hearing of Annie's recovery, Dylan had discounted the special experience which seemed to have triggered it.

"This is all a bit strange" had been his comment on being told of it by Auntie Maggie. Here, though, he was struck by Annie's tone; touched by her earnestness and moved by her sincerity.

"Honestly, she'd said," thought Dylan, "If Annie is anything she's honest."

The word wove a web of credence. Dylan was engaged; he considered what she'd just said.

"If she was so sure at the time, something special must have taken place. Regardless of what happened today, she made some kind of connection at the spring… and then kept it up with her visits to the lych-gate."

"Annie, when you sat in the lych-gate, what were those peaceful feelings like?"

She told him what she'd told Auntie Maggie a few days earlier.

"And they happened every time you were there?"

"Almost."

Dylan nodded pensively.

"I'll come back and see you soon."

In the kitchen, three expectant faces were told that Annie was low.

"She's upset about everything but the main problem is that she's sure now that she made up her relationship with St Cennydd, so obviously she can't expect him to support her anymore," and turning to Auntie Maggie he continued, "I'll talk to you tomorrow about visiting the doctor, OK?"

"Why not now?"

"Well, Annie said some things, Auntie Maggie, and I need more time to think about them."

Auntie Maggie was about to speak but in the end said nothing; her questioning stare said it all, though. Before long the family dispersed, to grieve for Arthur the best that they could.

# TWENTY-FIVE

IT WAS LUNCHTIME the next day. The wind had swung to the south-west, bringing with it changeable weather; for the next several days, showers were forecasted, some of them heavy. Dylan parked his rental car at the east end of Llangennydd church in the same spot as the day before... tidily this time, though. Today, no legging it through the lych-gate; rather, he chose to sit there.

His day had begun with a decision to forgo the office, but Annie would have none of it.

"I've decided," she'd said sadly, "that I've got to force myself to get back into the same routine with the children. And don't be upset now Dylan but I think it'll be easier today if I'm on my own."

"All right, Annie," he'd replied, "but I'll just go in for the morning. I'm sure your mother could use my help with arranging the funeral. I'll stop and talk to her about it on the way to work."

At his office, Dylan had gone over Annie's plea the previous evening.

"What do I know about spiritual experiences? Something special must have happened, though, because Annie was so sure of it at the time. And whatever it was actually healed her... and naturally. It's amazing, but why would it all change?"

During the morning he'd gone over this several times and had become increasingly comfortable with Annie's assertion: "I was certain I was blessed by a spirit at the spring. I was, honestly." And if she had been blessed, it made no sense to him that it would end in a mess like this.

All this till Auntie Maggie had come to mind, and in particular her reminder last night that Annie's time was up, followed by her piercing, questioning stare. In the face of this, Dylan had wavered.

"Am I making more than I should of what Annie said? I don't think so! Obviously, I'll never know what happened at the spring but Annie really was healed by something. It seems a shame to give up on it so easily, especially when the thought of her visiting her doctor makes me uneasy."

That's when he'd decided to visit Llangennydd church on the way home and walk in Annie's footsteps, so to speak; hence his presence at the lych-gate at lunchtime.

As he sat there, he imagined the instant when Annie on this very spot had become aware that she wasn't depressed. In a while, he crossed the road, knelt at the spring, cupped his hands and drank, and imagined her lightness when she felt that she'd been touched. Then, back to the gate where he fingered the carving with the gulls; he imagined Annie's ecstasy when she recognised this as a sign. Seated in the lych-gate again, he imagined her thrill on being embraced by that peaceful feeling and identifying it with the spirit. The emotions that she'd gone through!

When he entered the church he sensed an aura, so that when he pictured Annie taking her leap of faith, the image came to life. He wondered whether she'd thought something to the effect of, "To heck with everything else; I'm just going to go for it!" The more he'd walked in Annie's footsteps, the more real her experiences had become. As he left the church, he imagined Annie's anguish on discovering that the surfer was a girl. Dylan shook his head; that footstep was hard to take.

Back on the seat in the lych-gate, he ran over their life together; she'd been so easy to love – she'd been brilliant.

you've supported her. Annie once said that if ever there was a saint, it's Dylan."

He smiled; 'twas too restrained to be quirky, though.

"Hello, Annie."

She was in her bedroom, she'd gone there rather than take her usual walk because she was exhausted after exerting herself trying to be as normal as possible with the children. She lay on her side on the counterpane.

"Hello, Dylan."

He was reminded of a broken reed: how could fifteen stupid minutes have led to this?

"Annie, you told me that you'd honestly thought that you'd been blessed by a spirit at the spring; it was a spiritual experience, if you like. Well, let me tell you that I believe you were blessed as well, and if you were, it makes no sense that it all would end like this."

Despite Dylan's firmness of mind in this attempt to revive Annie, he was nervous, for what he was doing had to be done right. He moved quietly from the chair to the end of the bed. Annie faced away from him.

"Everything that happened after that experience followed in a positive way from it, until your last dream; so it seems to me Annie that the only explanation for this awful outcome is that you misinterpreted that dream. Your view of it has to be wrong, because it doesn't fit the facts. No saint would set you up like this."

It surprised Dylan that he'd so easily embedded himself into Annie's world; after all, he'd only been involved for a day. He wished that she'd respond, though.

"So I have to believe, Annie, that the surfer... the disciple in your dream... was not introduced by St Cennydd as someone

"I know Auntie Maggie disagrees but to me it seems ridiculous to give up on whatever it was that healed her. So what I need to do now is persuade Annie to get in touch with the spirit again; persuade her to come back here and experience that same peaceful feeling. That won't happen though while she thinks she made the whole thing up. So I'll just have to convince her somehow that her experience was real."

Once more he ran through the saga of Annie and St Cennydd from the spirit at the spring to the surfer as a spoiler. Dylan pictured Sarah yesterday slumped in a pew in front of him. He hardly knew her, but well enough to feel that no spoiler was she; an incongruity which encouraged his train of thought.

"What is a spiritual experience, anyway? Does a miracle take place, one which actually shifts a person to a different plane, or is there a trick of the imagination which goes hand in hand with an actual event? I've no idea, but from what I hear, they do happen. So, let's accept that Annie's experience at the spring was spiritual; the rest of her story follows naturally and positively from that... except for that last dream in which St Cennydd handed her a baby. So she should scrap that dream then. Not a chance, I'm afraid! Its impact was too powerful and it's timing spot on. What's more the surfer in the dream was essential in the build up to Annie's leap of faith. Hmm! That's right! So perhaps Annie should look at the dream in a different light... well, yes, of course, that's it! That would do it; that interpretation would fit the facts... and might be a way for me to try to convince Annie that her experience was real after all."

For a moment, however, Dylan sat still in the lych-gate and gazed abstractedly. Why? In light of an apparent revelation, why was he not expressing relief? Because the way in which he now saw that Annie could reconnect with the spirit might eventually result in disagreeable consequences for him. But as these were uncertain and remote while Annie's need, in his mind, was clear cut and pressing, his enthusiasm resurged almost immediately. Optimism held sway – until second-guessing set in.

"Can you really hang your hat on this idea?"

"Come on, you know I can't completely," Dylan chuckled, "It's just an idea… but that's not the point. Listen! The thing is Annie was definitely healed by something… something generous, obviously; it wouldn't be something that would give with one hand and take away with the other, so all she needs to do is get in touch with it again. That's my priority now, and if Annie accepts my idea, she has a chance… a chance to get well again. To be honest, it doesn't matter if I can't hang my hat on it… as long as Annie can."

"What if she can't, though?"

Images of Annie suffering and his partial responsibility for it made it imperative that this wavering be stopped. On the seat in the lych-gate, the improbable aspects of his idea became irrelevant in the face of the possibility of giving Annie another chance.

Now, he had to describe his idea to Auntie Maggie. He was sure she would resist, but he had to tell her: it would be disrespectful not to.

"I don't like it, Dylan. I don't like it all."

Auntie Maggie was in Annie's house: she'd agreed to be there by noon, just in case Annie needed time to herself. She looked worried as she spoke

"We've been here before, you see. For a whole week, I struggled with a dilemma; back and forth I went with Annie… should I restrain her or sustain her… and the moment I sort it out, here you are bringing it up again. You mustn't do it, Dylan. What happened yesterday was a blessing in disguise. It's not

pretty, I know, but her infatuation with St Cennydd need to be quashed, and if she can't deal with the fallout on h own, then she needs to see her doctor. We had an agreemen remember? You know your new idea won't come to anything anyway, except another disappointment for Annie. I'm telling you, Dylan, you shouldn't encourage this."

Dylan had expected her to resist, but so fierce a resistance was still surprising. By the time he'd arrived home, however, he'd completely committed to his idea, so there was no chance Auntie Maggie could deter him. And yet, out of respect, he couldn't dismiss her. He reasoned gently.

"Auntie Maggie, I understand your concern, and as for the doctor, he probably wouldn't be able to see her before Monday anyway. Look, you must agree that Annie made some sort of connection at the spring? And it healed her? All I'm trying to do is give her a chance to make that connection again. After that, I honestly don't know what to expect. Perhaps you're right that nothing will come of it, but shouldn't we give it a go?"

Auntie Maggie assumed a sadder and more reflective tone.

"You know that I wanted above all for Annie to be happy. I hated the thought of her relapsing, so I made the mistake of shielding her from reality for too long. Now, you're about to try and do the same."

"Don't you think her experience was spiritual?"

"I don't know, Dylan," sadly again, "Do you?"

"Yes, I do by now, mainly because she herself thought so… and with such conviction."

"Regardless," Auntie Maggie continued, "It hurts to see her this way. She's like a daughter to me, as you know," and tears came to her eyes. She let Dylan hug her for quite a while, and on recovering she said, "I do admire you though for the way

who'd be the father of your child," and here, involuntarily, Dylan inwardly winced, "but as a person who'd be your guide, someone who would lead you to the saint's surrogate; and if I'm right about that, Annie, you don't have to think anymore that you made your spiritual experience up... it was as real as you thought it was at the time."

How was it that Dylan could readily speak, with only an occasional wince, of his Annie making love to another man? It followed from a form of epiphany which he'd experienced earlier at the lych-gate. At the time, he'd been reasonably optimistic that his interpretation of Annie's dream could reunite her with the spirit, but as for Sarah as a guide after that, he'd had little conviction, and anyway he hadn't dwelt on it: getting Annie to experience that warm feeling again – giving her another chance – had been his priority. He had decided, however, that should Annie by some unimaginable miracle become pregnant with St Cennydd's baby, he would condone her adultery: he was sure that he'd be able to view it not as an act of infidelity, not as a slap to his face, but as an essential step to Annie regaining her health. Also, relegating his feelings to hers, should the occasion arise, would surely help rid his conscience of the Marlborough lapse and more to the point its devastating consequences. And in any case, no self-sacrifice would be too great should it lead to the resurrection of his relationship with Annie. At that same time, he'd also decided that his interpretation of Annie's dream should be presented with enthusiasm and conviction, for onto the slightest hesitation Annie would surely latch.

He concluded his case with, "You see, Annie, my view of your dream fits the facts; it doesn't call for Sarah the surfer to be a boy."

Still no response from Annie; Dylan fraught with frustration!

He'd assumed that she'd embrace his idea. God forbid that the proverbial brick wall was in his face already. He crept around the bed and knelt in front of Annie.

"Please speak to me, Annie."

Lifeless were her eyes when they opened. She spoke monotonously with no emotion.

"It's not that I'm ungrateful, but it's no use, Dylan. You're clutching at straws. This new idea regarding the surfer will come to nothing too, and I can't take another let down."

When earlier Auntie Maggie had voiced similar sentiments, they had been deflected by Dylan; for the plausibility of his idea had taken a back seat to his main objective: that of reconnecting Annie with the spirit in the hope that she'd be healed as before. Now, however, with Annie echoing Auntie Maggie's scepticism, Dylan failed to deflect this time and second-guessing resurfaced.

"Am I getting in over my head? I've no reason to believe that Sarah will turn out to be a guide, so am I playing with fire pushing my idea on Annie? Perhaps Auntie Maggie is right that all I'm doing is setting her up for another huge disappointment. Should I back off then? No, no, no, no! You must persuade her to go back to the lych-gate. What has she got to lose? Either that feeling will embrace her and she'll recover again, or it won't… and then I'll take Annie to the doctor on Monday."

Dylan rallied himself to remain upbeat. He took Annie's hands and inched closer to her face; he pleaded with passion.

"Think about it, Annie. What saint would inflict this crisis on you? You must have gone wrong somewhere. I've told you what I think, and surely you agree that my explanation of your dream gives you a chance to get back on track?"

Dylan backed off a bit.

"It won't work," whispered Annie, "and anyway I can't even

think about being unfaithful to you again. I couldn't do that to you, Dylan," with more liveliness now. Dylan's riposte was immediate.

"Not to me, Annie," with the emphasis on "to", "but for me," and he earnestly described his own pressing need for redemption.

"Please do it for me as well. You'd be giving me a second chance."

The baring of a soul invariably touches another. Annie freed her hands, pushed up and rested on her elbow; her face was full of expression now.

"As I just said, it's no use. You see, the bottom line is that I'm sure I've lost my connection with the spirit… if I ever had one."

"Come on, Annie! You only think that because you've convinced yourself that you've made this whole thing up. I've just shown you that you didn't. You thought at the time that your experience at the spring was real. Well, Annie, it was. What's more, is your saint so fickle? Not from what I've heard," and to maintain momentum, he took a gamble, rashly really, for he hadn't weighed the odds.

"Let's go to the church, Annie," as he gestured energetically, "Let's go now, so that you can see how wrong you are."

"It won't happen, Dylan. I won't get that peaceful feeling anymore."

Nor could Dylan be sure that she would, but there was no turning back now. He took her one free hand.

"Annie, why would you be handpicked by St Cennydd only then to be dumped without an explanation? You will get that feeling, Annie. Come on! Take another leap of faith. It'll be easier this time, because you'll know you have my blessing."

"You're rushing me, Dylan."

"I know I am, but that's what St Cennydd would want me to do, don't you think?"

Annie stared at him suspiciously. Dylan could read her mind: she was almost certainly wondering whether he was making fun of her.

At tipping points, a push is preferable to persuasion... at times, and this was such an occasion, Dylan had decided. With the swagger of one whose deal is done he rose abruptly and aimed for the door.

"Come on, Annie, get up. Wear one of your green tops... the waterproof one just in case, and make sure you'll be warm enough. I'll talk to Auntie Maggie."

As he left, he wasn't certain of Annie's cooperation, but sufficiently so to engage her aunt. She, to the shaking of her noble head and shows of much frustration, agreed to care for Connie and Connor while their mother and father sought salvation.

# TWENTY-SIX

THERE ARE SCENES that are showstoppers; one such stuns motorists at the top of the hill which overlooks Llangennydd. From there, movement, depth and colour combine to create awe. A yellow car stopped at that spot on this Friday afternoon; its engine was left running.

"What if it doesn't happen, Dylan?"

This regular refrain from Annie during their journey had pinned Dylan to his cheerleading hat. He'd hardly touched on the improbable aspects of his interpretation of Annie's dream; sustaining his enthusiasm for this visit to the church had monopolised his energies.

"Annie, don't worry now. You've had that feeling before and you'll have it again. St Cennydd won't let you down… I know it!"

On those occasions when he'd felt a need to reassure himself, his doubts had been dismissed and he'd forced himself to focus on Annie instead: it was imperative that she not sense any wavering on his part.

He'd stopped at the top of the hill hoping to elevate Annie's spirits.

"Isn't it gorgeous up here?" and then down the hill they drove, relinquishing the view. As they turned towards the village green, Dylan remarked, "I'd rather not drop you right next to the church."

Annie's head wheeled, her expression cloaked in enquiry.

"It's just that I'd prefer you to walk from the caravan park. Is that all right with you?"

Annie nodded in a way that made it clear she understood his line of reasoning. Later, he bade her goodbye.

"Annie, I'll pick you up in forty-five minutes. Don't worry now! Everything will go well," while to himself he prayed that no rain would fall and possibly put a damper on the visit.

With Annie on her way to the church, Dylan relaxed... and immediately felt drained. No wonder: all day his mind had turned over at a frenetic pace. Out of the blue, Auntie Maggie's comments earlier in the afternoon came to mind.

"You know your idea won't come to anything anyway, except another disappointment for Annie."

Despite his lassitude, Dylan vigorously defended his decision to encourage Annie to try to connect with the spirit. Had he done nothing, she'd be destined to visit her doctor on Monday.

"This way, though, if she experiences that peaceful feeling, Annie's self-confidence is bound to bounce back; she'll be buoyant again. I admit I don't know what to expect after that. Still, what does Annie have to lose?"

But Auntie Maggie's words would not be rebuffed; they came back at Dylan, and he, tired and with time on his hands, found it hard to deflect them.

"... except another disappointment for Annie."

Dylan was cornered; he was forced for the first time to seriously consider the consequences should Annie reconnect with the spirit at the lych-gate. He admitted to himself that it was probably unlikely that Sarah would turn out to be Annie's guide; he even pictured them meeting... Sarah perplexed and Annie severely disappointed.

"But there's a good chance that they'll never meet, even if Annie goes looking for her."

In that case, wouldn't Annie have it both ways? Wouldn't she then maintain her relationship with the saint without having to satisfy his outrageous request?

But then Dylan challenged himself with, "Realistically, though, how long can I expect Annie to have faith in my idea without something happening?"

He couldn't answer that, but at least it would buy time just in case something else cropped up.

"But what could that be?" in a plaintive tone.

The more he delved, the harder it became not to question his wisdom in pressing Annie to pursue his idea.

"Yes, Dylan, what could that be?"

A brainwave pierced this onset of doubt. It struck him that at some point St Cennydd might confirm to Annie, in a dream perhaps, that his request really had been a test, and then assured her that she'd already passed it. After all, Annie had made it clear that she intended to obey the saint and as a result may have done enough to demonstrate to his satisfaction her loyalty and devotion. Under this scenario, he would expect no more from her; she'd already earned his support and goodwill.

"Dylan, Dylan, come on now! Stop it! This is getting ridiculous."

Had Dylan known his Bible, he might not have been as dismissive, for his big idea had a biblical precedent: Abraham being commanded by God in Genesis to sacrifice his son Isaac. As it was, no such connection was made; Dylan stepped back into his car, slowly shaking his head.

"Jesus! I hope I'm not setting Annie up for another fall. Even if she's embraced by that feeling, I'm beginning to think that all I may have done is buy time for her."

He suddenly became irritated.

"This arguing is pointless. I'd be much better off waiting until I know what happens to Annie at the lych-gate."

He spent the next twenty minutes struggling to heed his own advice.

Dylan had parked up the street where Trevor had hidden the day before. He walked slowly towards the church, his emotions churning. Close to the village green, Dylan peeped around a building, much as Trevor had done. There was Annie, seated in the lych-gate, glancing repeatedly in his direction. She spotted him, rose, and approached. He thought her more beautiful than he'd ever thought before.

Composed, her appearance,
Her head was held high,
But the crux was a smile
Which was curiously shy.

"I told you, didn't I, Annie?"

She nodded and came closer. He was touched when she faced him from a few feet away, still smiling shyly, sizing him up and down, and thrilled then to be embraced by her. He reciprocated with relief and joy; his emotions which earlier had churned now aligned themselves into love of Annie.

"Dylan," she whispered, "Are you sure you want me to pursue this? You don't mind if I do this to you?"

At a time when Dylan was becoming increasingly uneasy with his idea, Annie's complete acceptance of it was momentarily unsettling. This distraction, however, was soon brushed aside and he refocused on Annie and her questions.

"Not to me, Annie, but for me. Do it for both of us, all right?"

He could hardly bear the pleasure when she squeezed him extra tightly. The feel of the skin of her face on his took his breath away. He'd imagined this reunion for weeks; it was as rich and rewarding as he'd hoped it would be. In the middle of the road not far from the spring, Annie cried quietly; Dylan stroked her hair.

In the wake of this tender reaffirmation of love and her reconnection with the spirit, Annie glowed; for a moment she found this disconcerting.

"For me, is the line really that thin between contentment and despair?"

But that's as far as her questioning went; the future had taken on an acceptable form. And what a relief it was to know that her experience at the spring had been real after all. Annie allowed herself optimism. Why did she do so this time, when in every previous recovery it had been crushed ruthlessly? Was tempting fate no longer a concern? It seemed not, but was she wise?

At home, she warmed to her family again, and in particular Auntie Maggie whom she knew she'd hurt terribly on Wednesday afternoon.

Annie felt calm as well, even while anticipating a most unseemly act. While the thought was uncomfortable, it held no fear, thanks to the saint's renewed support and, now, Dylan's blessing. She marvelled at how calm she was, as calm as she'd felt a few days earlier after taking her leap of faith, but how dissimilar the two experiences! This time, she was herself, very much the Annie of old. With Dylan at her elbow, no call for rationalisation, no need for subterfuge. Her unconventional act would be above board and its consequences unchallenging; this time her feet were firmly on the ground, unlike the previous occasion when somehow she'd thrown her inhibitions and flown in another world, and in the process upset Auntie Maggie.

So, Annie's immediate priority was to make amends with her aunt; with her head to one side in apology, she approached Auntie Maggie.

"The spirit is still my friend, Auntie Maggie. I know that upsets you, but may I hug you, anyway… please?"

Auntie Maggie, with a pained expression, shook her noble head.

"It's hard for me, Annie, I'm so sorry."

"Auntie Maggie, I understand, and I'm sorry too. I don't know what came over me on Wednesday, but now I'm fine, I promise."

Auntie Maggie came to life, her face assumed incredulity.

"How can you say that, Annie, when you're still going through with this nonsense?"

Annie would not be deflected.

"But it's different now with Dylan at my side. You can surely see that?"

Auntie Maggie's face softened; warmth and sadness mingled.

"It's good to see you happy again, Annie, but at the same time I'm worried for you. You're playing with fire, you know. I've got to go now," and she bade goodbye to all four individually.

Annie yearned for Auntie Maggie's approval, so she was disappointed, and yet undaunted, now with the spirit and Dylan in tandem, a formidable force in her favour. Next in line for affection were the children. She knelt by them and beamed. Then, while in a hug, she noticed Dylan deep in thought.

"Oh! The poor thing! This isn't as easy for him as he's been letting on. Just the thought of what I'm going to do must get him down sometimes; but from what he says anyway, he's adamant that I should go through with it."

So, on an extraordinary mission Annie seemed set fair.

Dylan's increasing unease with his idea had been washed away by the warmth of Annie's reception at the village green; his worries had been overrun by the joy engendered by her recovery and the passion released by reunion. Those moments had been magical, they'd enthralled, and yet, despite their residual glow, Dylan was on the defensive again by late afternoon: for if all he'd done was buy Annie time, a repeat of those highs was unlikely. By now he'd accepted that it was unrealistic to expect Sarah to turn out to be Annie's guide.

"After all, why should she be?" he'd conceded, "I shouldn't have pressed Annie to…"

"Dylan," he chastised himself, "Don't be so silly! Look at her over there with the children! She's so full of confidence that I wouldn't put anything past her. So how can you possibly regret what you did?"

He waved at Annie. She smiled at him shyly, in the same way as earlier in the day; it was as if she was ashamed of having made a fuss. Then he acknowledged Peggy who'd just arrived. She looked sad; her loss was obviously sinking in.

Dylan reverted to a familiar rationalisation: it made no sense that a saint would set someone up to be crushed; there had to be – just had to be – some way acceptable to Annie of translating her spiritual experience into a happy outcome.

"But what could that be, Dylan?" plaintively, "What could it be?"

The same old roadblock had re-emerged.

"So all I've done is buy Annie time? Hmmm! It could be quite some time, I suppose."

Dylan determined to put on a good face. The last time he'd tried to do so with Annie was following the incident in the lift. It had proven to be surprisingly difficult. Still, it was imperative that Annie not gather an inkling of his internal struggle, especially during the time leading up to Arthur's funeral: a relapse by Annie while the others grieved would be awful.

He looked at Annie again; she was ardently consoling Peggy. God, he loved her, but to think what they'd been through together! She glanced at Dylan and screwed up her face, expressing sorrow for her mother, and then she smiled, shyly again.

"While she's like this," thought Dylan, "I can at least be sure that Auntie Maggie won't be reminding me that her niece's time is up."

# TWENTY-SEVEN

EARLY THAT SAME evening in the kitchen at Annie's house, the family gathered again; all were aware, by now, of the latest twist in Annie's tale. The children weren't in bed yet: they were being encouraged to talk about their granddad. He's gone to heaven, they'd been told. In various ways, all present had been close to Arthur, and found kind and humorous things to say. Reactions to anecdotes gave proof that emotions, and Peggy's in particular, weren't far beneath the surface. Following one sobbing episode, she turned to Annie.

"I'm glad you're feeling better about your father."

Annie smiled appreciatively.

"Thanks. Everything seemed so bleak last night."

Presumably moved by that memory and keen to really connect again, Annie proceeded to do the rounds. She embraced her mother, who broke into tears once more. Then, holding Auntie Maggie's hands, she whispered, though all could hear what she said, "I wouldn't have made it without you... honest to God. I can't tell you how much I owe you."

Auntie Maggie, clearly still somewhat withdrawn, may have deflected this heartfelt admission under different circumstances, but now she too succumbed... and wept. Trevor, however, held out, although multiple adjustments to spectacles and tie did hint at mounting emotion. Next, the children, who made no bones about their joy at having their mother back again.

Then, out of the blue, "Will you come outside with me, Dylan?"

He glanced at the others, shrugged his shoulders, and complied.

Clouds had closed in and it was raining lightly so they got no further than the back porch; Dylan's hands were taken.

"I feel so close to you, Dylan, but if you don't mind, I'd prefer that we didn't sleep together until this business is behind us. Is that OK with you?"

Dylan half-smiled, nodded, and hugged her. Now it was her turn to cry, while he gazed abstractedly at rainwater worming its way down the window panes.

Next morning, a Saturday, Annie sought the surfer. No sign of her in Llangennydd church, but a peaceful feeling embraced her. Its dependability buoyed Annie and convinced her that sooner or later the surfer would appear and reveal. Next, she supped at the spring, and then aimed for the surfers' beach. In her waterproof green top, she walked with a bounce in her step. At the beach, she perched on a dune and peered seaward.

"Hmm! I don't see her anywhere. I wonder if the surrogate could be one of those surfers."

Remarkably, this concept was considered without qualm, for she saw herself as a piece in a grand, symbiotic design, in which she was being enabled, by Dylan and the spirit of St Cennydd, to achieve a lofty goal; one that would also benefit her enablers in equal measure. Her feet were stripped of socks and shoes; she slowly approached the seashore. Oh! How chilly the water felt! When a surfer waved, her interest leapt, only to wane in a while when he plopped in the water well short of her, paddled away with gusto, not to wave again.

"Probably overcome by shyness," was Annie's take on that.

She arrived home to a welcome from Connie and Connor and a questioning look from Dylan. She shook her head unobtrusively and at the first opportunity gave him a long embrace. The evening was spent with all the family, reminiscing of Arthur and discussing arrangements for the funeral which now they knew would take place on Tuesday. On Sunday, Annie repeated the same routine, but again with a negative result. So confident was she, however, of her connection with the spirit that on Monday she chose not to visit the church. During the morning she alternated between consoling her mother and consulting the undertaker. Auntie Maggie took care of the children; Dylan had gone back to work for a day.

At noon, Annie left for the beach and settled across from the surfers. As before, one in the distance waved. She hurried to the shoreline as the surfer boogied his board with panache. This time, he threw her a glance, before paddling back to the breakers.

"He's definitely the same one as last time… grayish wet suit and fairly tall, nice-looking and open-faced and all. Could he be the one? Does he have a special air about him?"

The runs were repeated; he was clearly showing off, and after each plop in the water, Annie caught his glance. Interestingly, though, when he and his fellow surfers left the beach, Annie was not acknowledged – shyness all over again?

"So, could he be the one? No, no, no! Don't jump the gun, Annie! I should wait to find out from… what's her name, again? Oh, yes… Sarah!"

When Dylan was told of this, he nodded thoughtfully with his lips compressed.

"Oh!" she sighed to herself, "This must be hard for him to take," but she couldn't resist persisting.

"Dylan, do you think he could be the one? Who knows… but never mind! Sarah will settle it one of these days. There's no rush, is there?"

Later, five adults met as before. Prompted by Trevor, surprisingly, each went over the roots of their rift with Arthur – rifts sadly unresolved at his death – and sought understanding from each other, and from God. Particularly moving was Auntie Maggie's narrative, wherein she mentioned her misgivings about Annie, and yet, opened her arms to her. So, it was as one they faced the day of the funeral.

Annie's account of the surfer showing off had naturally troubled Dylan. Her conviction that Sarah would be her guide made him wince; he felt a fraud. Though admittedly in good faith, he had led her up a blind alley, and sooner or later she'd discover that Sarah couldn't help. How would Annie cope, he wondered, and would she blame him? Auntie Maggie had been right to recommend she bite the bullet.

"No, no, no! Don't say that! Even if all you've done is buy her time. Just look at her now – calm and contented."

A burst of affection cleansed him of much of his guilt. He slid along the floor and knelt at her feet; brown eyes locked on very blue. She blessed him with her classic smile; in response, his quirky. Then, on her lap he laid his head, which led to such sweet nothings.

# TWENTY-EIGHT

IT WAS ALMOST noon; Arthur's memorial service was drawing to a close in Rhossili's little church. In the left front pew sat the children, comically dwarfed on either side by Trevor and Auntie Maggie; opposite, Peggy sat, flanked by Dylan and Annie. During the service, they'd shown little emotion; most of theirs had been spent at the crematorium earlier in the day. There, in private, the children absent and accompanied only by Dylan's parents, they'd wept their farewells.

The minister spoke a final solemn word. Then, to an organ lament, the family filed down the aisle. First, Peggy, hand in hand with Connie and Connor; by them, in pew after pew, most were charmed, and many moved. The congregation's gossips were agog, for Annie and Dylan held hands as well; so what were the odds of a connection, then, between their reunion and Arthur's demise? Auntie Maggie's arm threaded Trevor's.

"Good God!" whispered Annie; Connie in front, cocked her head.

"What's the matter?" from Dylan, naturally concerned.

As she spoke, Annie looked straight ahead.

"Don't look now but to the left at the back is the surfer; she's doing her best to hide her face. Her name's Sarah, right? I've got to talk to her, Dylan, but I must go outside now and do some greeting with Mammy... so will you go and sit with her? Make sure she comes to Auntie Maggie's house for something to eat and a cup of tea. She probably won't want to mix, so take her to Trevor's study. I'll talk to her there... but later. Will you do that?"

Dylan was floored. His chest tightened; he was forced to take a deep breath.

"Jesus! So this is it!" he thought, "The moment of truth is here. I thought I had bought her more time than this."

While he had no choice but to walk slowly down the aisle, much in his make-up picked up pace, including his heartbeat – and thoughts.

"Can I avoid asking Sarah to meet Annie? No, no, I have to do it, but I could pretend that Sarah refused. Hmmm! Given the way I am with Annie, I know I couldn't pull that off, and anyway, I'm in deep enough water as it is."

He then changed tack.

"Think of poor Annie! How will she deal with all this, I wonder? Perhaps I can persuade her to go back to the church and connect with the spirit again. No, I don't think that'll work. I'm afraid this disappointment will shatter her faith once and for all."

Dylan was diverted from his train of thought by a natural empathy which forced him to focus on the surfer's expression.

"God, she looks scared, like an animal trapped in a headlight. I've got to calm her, somehow."

As he carefully stepped around Sarah, he was struck by her dazzling blonde hair. He then sat on the pew beside her. Dylan's mind was distracted by Auntie Maggie's incredulous stare; he had to force himself to concentrate on Sarah.

"Hello," very quietly with gentleness and warmth, "It's nice to meet you again, but I'm surprised to see you here."

Thankfully, he noticed an improvement in her demeanour already.

"So you're related to the man who died?" she whispered.

Dylan nodded, and added, "He was Annie's father… Annie, my wife, you know?"

There was no response from Sarah, who drew flitting, curious glances from many filtering by.

"Do you mind if I ask you why you're here?" said Dylan.

"No, I don't mind," she replied, whispering still, "It's just that I've felt partly responsible for his death," to Dylan's remonstrations, "So when I saw a funeral notice, I guessed it might be his. I decided that being here might help me, help me overcome my guilt."

"Sarah, Sarah," immediately from Dylan, "How can you be blamed for just stumbling into a family affair?" and he repeated an earlier line, "If it was stress that killed him, then he brought it upon himself."

He wondered if the time was right for raising Annie's request. He exhaled; he cringed at the thought of what he was about to put in motion, but it had to be done. He acknowledged that he'd been skating on thin ice. Auntie Maggie had been right: it was time for Annie to bite the bullet. He gazed at Sarah; he thought her pretty, petite... and vulnerable.

"Perhaps there's no need to involve her in this. Why put her through it?"

He knew deep down, however, that clear-cut closure for Annie demanded a showdown with Sarah.

"Sarah," gently, in hushed tones, but in earnest, "Would you agree to meet Annie, my wife? She'd like to talk to you."

"Why?"

"I think it's better if that comes from her. She'll be at Auntie Maggie's house soon for a cup of tea with the mourners. She'd like you to meet her there in a private room. There's no need for you to mix at all."

Sarah's face gave little away.

"Perhaps you think that she's angry at you," he offered, "but I can tell you that she's not. She just wants to ask you a question, that's all."

To his surprise, Sarah whispered, "If you promise she's not angry, I will meet her."

Dylan couldn't bring himself to thank her, but he vowed to consider and protect her feelings in the run-up to her meeting with Annie – and during it, if need be.

Fortunately, the rain in the forecast had held off; so no scurrying or scattering for shelter as mourners emerged from the church. The post-funeral gathering at Auntie Maggie's house, though held to honour and reflect upon Arthur, was abuzz with talk of Sarah. Not for the first time, she'd spoilt his day and, as before, without meaning to do so. It was natural that the mourners and the gossips in particular wondered who she was. A few had heard that Annie had met this stranger on a walk along the beach. But why had Dylan indulged her so? Stranger still, why was she closeted in the study? The majority of those present, however, were sufficiently polite to avoid appearing curious. In fact, many expressed their sadness that a grieving family should suffer from such a distraction; as for others, though, no such nicety. These now huddled around a couple who held forth, repeating snippets they'd overheard of Dylan's chat with Sarah in the church; some of them mysterious, they reported, suggesting that she may have had some dealings with Arthur. It was this group too which openly and piously opined that it was an awful shame that such a striking girl should be lame. Suddenly, though, all decorum was dispensed with; every head, in unison, turned towards the study where Annie gently knocked upon the door. She entered, and soon after, Dylan came out to an unsettling and, it seemed to him, expectant hush.

"Annie and her friend want to chat... that's all!" he announced, to no one in particular. Unsurprisingly, this effort failed to satisfy; speculation persisted, and manifestly so in several huddles. Regardless, Dylan circulated, gamely reassuring his parents, Peggy, Auntie Maggie and Trevor that Annie was all right. When pumped for more details, however, he doggedly stuck to his line. By now, he regretted exposing, even if in part, their fantastical family affair.

"But what could I have done? I had to respect Annie's request."

For ten minutes, those gathered snacked and supped, and gossiped in many cases. Some regularly glanced at the door of the study, but none as frequently as Auntie Maggie. Clearly agitated, she cornered Dylan. Though her expression in general was enigmatic, when she fretted, it was not.

"I realise that you'd rather not tell me, Dylan, but I do need to know what's going on. Please tell me what's happening. Is she really going through with this?"

Dylan felt for her: she'd invested so much in Annie. He could put her mind at rest and tell her that nothing would come of this meeting. But she'd know soon enough, anyway.

"Dylan!"

This was spoken with urgency from the study. Annie's tone was ominous; Dylan tensed. Despite this, he took Auntie Maggie's hands, and with his eyes on hers whispered, "I'll talk to you about it soon, I promise."

He made for the study door, deliberately avoiding all eye contact.

The scene that met Dylan was in line with his expectations: Annie clearly frustrated and panicky, Sarah obviously bemused and upset. Once the door was shut, Annie gave vent.

"Dylan, she's no idea what I'm talking about."

"Shush, Annie! Keep your voice down. There's no need for the village to know."

"But, Dylan," spoken as urgently as before but quietly now, "I thought there'd be some little sign, but no! Nothing! She's been... Sarah's been sweet and understanding but totally unhelpful. I've told her what she needs to know, but it seems to mean nothing to her. I don't know what else to say."

Dylan had known for days that it would come to this, so why prolong the matter? But reason is one thing, instinct another, especially in one as sensitive as Dylan.

"It would be better if I wasn't abrupt," he thought.

So the play took on another scene, wherein Annie would be weaned, but gently and circuitously, from the notion of Sarah as her guide. He knelt by Annie's chair, held her hand, and spoke, "You shouldn't be surprised, Annie, that Sarah's not aware that she's meant to be your guide."

Then, to Sarah, "Are you sure you don't have anything to say to Annie? What about those men you surf with? Have you been struck by anything one of them may have done... or said, recently? Think hard, Sarah!"

Apologetic was she in reply.

"I am so sorry but there isn't anything, honestly! Anyway, I don't have much to do with them; you see, I'm not comfortable with men," and turning to Annie, spoke earnestly, "You are so lucky – your husband is..."

But Annie, apparently, had heard enough. She brushed Dylan's hands aside, and wildly waving her own, interrupted Sarah with, "It's no use, Dylan. She can't help me."

Dylan watched as she gesticulated. Her grimaces spoke of pain. Then, suddenly, Annie's face froze. In this pose she enquired of Sarah, "What were you going to say?"

Sarah had obviously been hurt by the earlier interruption, so this time she spoke more guardedly.

"I was going to say that you are very lucky: your husband is the nicest man I've known."

Annie's face remained frozen, as if nothing of import had been said. Meanwhile, Dylan cringed with embarrassment.

"What on earth made Sarah say that?" he asked himself, "She hardly knows me. And what's wrong with Annie? She looks dazed."

Astonishment followed as Annie relaxed, glanced at Dylan, knelt by Sarah, laid her head on the surfer's lap, and cried.

"You're an angel," Annie mumbled fitfully, "I'm so ashamed that I doubted you."

She then turned her head and smiling and sobbing gently, asked, "Did you hear what she just said, Dylan?"

Dylan nodded and repeated Sarah's phrase.

"Your husband is the nicest man I've known."

"Come on, Dylan! She couldn't be clearer than that, could she?"

Only then did Dylan's penny drop: sceptics aren't tuned to see the light, but when Dylan did, lightness coursed throughout his being as if a boulder had been lifted off his chest, as if he'd left his own body and was light enough to fly.

"Your husband is the nicest man I've known."

Dylan shook his head; it seemed that Sarah had turned up trumps, after all – just like that, when he'd least expected it. He reflected in wonder on this innocent remark which he saw might change their lives, and it had all come down to faith – Annie's faith: her conviction that she was blessed by a spirit at the spring and more recently that Sarah would point her to St Cennydd's surrogate. Whether her faith was a source of strength or sign of weakness, it had worked for Annie today, enabling her to be receptive to Sarah's words.

"Your husband is the nicest man I've known."

"Should I have seen this coming?" Dylan asked himself, "No! How could I have? Happy endings are one thing, but…"

It was likely now that Annie would be herself again and at the same time his conscience would be cleansed of guilt – and all this without enduring a most unseemly act. Of St Cennydd's role in this miracle, Dylan was ambivalent: he knew only that following Annie's experience at the spring, anything short of her redemption made no sense. A lovely cameo followed: Dylan witnessed the confusion on Sarah's face morph into understanding… and soon, into joy; for the first time he saw her smile.

Auntie Maggie's fretful face came to Dylan's mind: she as much as anyone was responsible for this. From the study door he motioned her to join him; a sea of silence parted, a troubled face drifted through. Naturally confused by the scene in the study, she repeatedly looked at Dylan, seeking an explanation.

He whispered more calmly than he felt, "The oracle has spoken, Auntie Maggie… and I'm the chosen one."

Confusion still on Auntie's Maggie's face: her penny too took time to drop. How many times did she glance back and forth between Annie and Sarah and Dylan before a smile warmed her face? Then, shaking her head, presumably in relief and lingering disbelief, she turned to face the little window and gazed at Burry Holm; this a prelude to embracing Dylan and releasing weeks of tension. It was the second time in a day that Dylan had seen her cry.

In a while, Sarah was introduced to Peggy and Trevor; they respectfully asked no questions, though they must have been dying to be put in the picture. Dylan's parents came next; not privy at all to Sarah's significance, they must have been bursting with curiosity as well, but they too curbed it. Later, as they left for home, Annie approached them. Her body language spoke of exhaustion; symptomatic was her hair, untrimmed and badly in need of care. And yet, her confident smile – and dimple – was proof that she was happy.

"Thanks for coming to Daddy's funeral. By the way, do you still have the camping equipment that we borrowed a long time ago? You do? Would it be all right if Dylan and I came to Tenby tomorrow and borrowed the stuff again?"

"Of course, but the forecast isn't very special for the next few days."

"Nothing will stop us taking the hike I have in mind."

Annie ignored their obvious bemusement and continued.

"I'd like to try and leave your house before lunch so we'd have to be with you by eleven. Here he comes! Don't say a thing – I haven't told him yet."

After the guests had dispersed, and while the women of the family tidied Auntie Maggie's house, Dylan gazed at Burry Holm… and figuratively pinched himself.

"Did it really happen?"

Though the intangibles in Annie's story were many, Dylan had been firm on one point: if indeed Annie's experience at the spring had been special, it wouldn't have made sense had it not led to a happy outcome, and in a way that was acceptable to her. Well, it seemed that it had, and all it had taken was for Annie to believe.

For the family, their farewell to Arthur had been marginalised by Sarah's innocent remark and its stunning and joyful effects; Dylan relished them over and over. Eventually, however, he was forced to address an aspect of the matter that was potentially troubling.

"I'll never understand Annie's connection with St Cennydd, and I can't share in her feelings for him either."

Here, he took a deep breath to calm himself.

"Still, I mustn't ever make light of their relationship. If I did, I'd be risking Annie's recovery... and mine."

He turned and glanced at the church; then his eyes lingered on their home.

"I just hope she's the same old Annie, that's all."

Early next morning, Annie and Dylan detoured to Llangennydd. It was he who'd suggested a rendezvous with the saint.

"You're right," she'd replied, "I should go to the lych-gate, but you know, I don't need that feeling, that reassurance, as much as before, now that I see St Cennydd's qualities in you."

Dylan had protested: this was just the type of thing he'd hoped that they'd have avoided.

"Come on, Annie! I feel funny when you say things like that. I'm the same person that I've always been, and I hope that you and I together will be the same as we were as well."

Annie had smiled with understanding; she stood, approached, and sat on his lap facing him. Then they'd hugged, and she'd laid her head on his shoulder.

"While I was ill that's all I wanted as well, Dylan. To me, our relationship has always been precious, too precious I think at times. As for St Cennydd, it's just comforting for me to know that he will give me strength if I get into trouble again. Think of him in that way, Dylan."

Here, Annie had released her embrace and lent back; their eyes met, brown locked on very blue.

"Now, we're going to have another baby, aren't we," she continued with a warm, open smile, "a baby... and I know you accept this... a baby which I have to believe is going to be born to remind people of St Cennydd's qualities and ideals; but the baby will still be ours, Dylan. We will make it... you and I."

She'd lent back further; her expression was empathetic and reassuring.

"Dylan, please don't worry! I promise you that St Cennydd will not come between us. And in any case, whenever I'll think of him, I'll also think of you" and here she'd laughed, "The funny thing is I've often said that if ever there was a saint, it's you."

This time, no demur from Dylan; it seemed his concerns had been addressed.

# EPILOGUE

ANNIE GAVE BIRTH one Friday evening. She was attended by a midwife, and Auntie Maggie of course; Dylan was there as well. Despite her exertions, she appeared to be alert.

"You needn't tell me. I know it's a boy," jokingly from Annie.

"How did you know?"

"Well, he has to be a boy, because we've already named him Kenny, haven't we Dylan?" and she teased with her smile, "Kenny O'Kinnon has a ring, don't you think?"

Dylan knew what was coming next; to him, throughout her pregnancy, Annie had repeatedly voiced a concern.

More serious now, Annie said, "Auntie Maggie?"

"Yes?"

"I want you tell me that his legs are all right."

"They're perfect, Annie… just perfect."

Annie smiled to herself and, turning towards Dylan, beckoned him to her side.

"Please phone Sarah," she whispered, "and tell her that. She'll want to know as well."

## Also by the author:

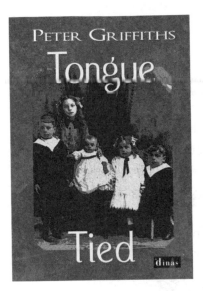

Tongue Tied opens in 1876 in North Wales with two young men who are firm friends. Soon, one has to leave for the South, but before they part they take part in an act of camaraderie: they each have a little red dragon tattooed on their left shoulder. All this takes a mere twelve pages and the whole of the rest of the book deals with the consequences of this act and its effect on the two families over the next three generations. In her review in *The Celtic Connection*, Mary Seaman wrote, "Intricate, multi-stranded end games yield a masterful conclusion." She ends her review with "Peter Griffiths' mystical novel *Tongue Tied* trills with grace notes on every page as it synchronises the harmonies of bloodlines and brotherhood in this sensational literary aria."

"*Tongue Tied* is a tale of what it means to be Welsh and should be on everyone's reading list, whether they've been to Wales or not, whether they are Welsh or not."

Lise Hull, *Ninnau*

"This is a novel that hinges on the small things that change lives – in this case a little red dragon – and the bigger things that change a culture, like industrialisation and the attendant mass migration to the South Wales Valleys."

Steve Dube, *Western Mail*

*The Mystical Milestone* is just one of a whole range of publications from Y Lolfa. For a full list of books currently in print, send now for your free copy of our new full-colour catalogue. Or simply surf into our website

## www.ylolfa.com

for secure on-line ordering.

y Lolfa

TALYBONT CEREDIGION CYMRU SY24 5HE
*e-mail* ylolfa@ylolfa.com
*website* www.ylolfa.com
*phone* (01970) 832 304
*fax* 832 782